# The Signposters

by the same author

\*

THE NIGHT-WATCHMEN

THE PIEMAKERS

WHERE THE WIND BLOWS

UP THE PIER

THE BEACHCOMBERS

THE OUTLANDERS

THE BONGLEWEED

# The Signposters

HELEN CRESSWELL

*Illustrated by*
GARETH FLOYD

FABER AND FABER LTD
3 Queen Square
London

First published in 1968
by Faber and Faber Limited
3 Queen Square London W.C.1
Reprinted 1969 and 1973
Printed in Great Britain by
Unwin Brothers Limited
The Gresham Press, Old Woking, Surrey


ISBN 0 571 08422 2

For my sister, Pauline, with love

# Preface

One of my hobbies is tracing back my ancestors. I have a weakness for family trees, inherited, no doubt, from Dyke Signposter, as you will understand when you have read this story. A year or two ago I traced myself back (more or less) on my maternal grandmother's side, to the Danby Rollers, and wrote about them in a book called *The Pie-makers*.

Now I have been lucky enough to unearth another document quite as interesting as the Danby Chronicles. I found it one wet afternoon in my grandfather Smith's library, tucked between Mrs Beeton and *Huckleberry Finn*.

My grandfather Smith told me that as far as he knew no one had ever read these papers because the writing was so bad, and the Smiths as a family had always been short-sighted and impatient of fine print. When I opened it, I saw with relief that the writing was not nearly so bad as my own, and I read it in an evening with no trouble at all.

It is quite clear to me that the people in this story were *my* ancestors. But if you care to think that they were yours, too, I shall not begrudge you your fancy. After all, anyone who has ever read a telephone directory will realize that we must all have *some* Smith in us, somewhere along the line.

# Chapter One

Barley Signposter could see for miles in all directions. And so she should be able to, she thought, puffing for breath. From the top of the hill she could look down over trees decorated with sharp new buds, and beyond that over fields greener than she could ever remember—because last spring, after all, had been a very long time ago.

Her sharp eyes picked out the road, but experience told her that this was not necessarily the right road. She wheeled slowly, like a weathercock, scanning the land, and sure enough, two more roads were spoking away from the hill. On one of them, tiny as a button, she saw what she was looking for. If you had asked Barley how she knew that this tiny, faceless speck was her father, she could not have told you for the world. But she had been born and bred on the roads, she had scanned from hills such as this a thousand times before, and she *did* know. Every trade has skills that cannot be taught.

Barley did not hurry back down the hill. Dyke was a mile or more away, and supper, she knew, would have to wait till his return. That was one of the things Hetty was very firm about.

"We may live like vagrants," she would say, "but we're

respectable folk, and we sit down to our meals like respectable folk. Meals is one thing can't be skimped."

She would be busy down there now at the bottom of the hill, working on the encampment. By the time Dyke was back and supper over, it would be too dark to move on to a village for the night. Besides, the tenting season had only just started, and the Signposters were usually

glad to lay their pillows on the turf after the long, house-bound winter.

Tonight would be the first camping out of the year, and all three of them had been parching for it for weeks now, ever since the grass had begun to drink the melting snow and shoot up tiny, impatient spears. Hetty, who sometimes became bored and moody while Dyke was away pacing, had been singing noisily all day and filling her apron with wild flowers for the sheer joy of it—for she hadn't a vase to put them in.

Pacing was the hardest part of Dyke's job, and the part that Hetty and Barley could not help him with at all. Their part was simply to wait. Every twenty years, by law, each road in Flockshire had to be re-paced and measured. If two villages were only a few miles apart, the job was done in a day or less. But sometimes the job took Dyke away for days on end. Flockshire was a big county —a tenth part of England, so they said—and you could walk for a day with never a hearth in sight.

Today's pacing had been only a small affair. The Sign-posters had left their winter quarters at Flock as dawn was breaking, and had reached the Straythorpe cross-roads by noon. There Dyke's signpost was still standing from last year, only slightly leaning after the buffeting of winter storms.

"Paint's worn well," Dyke had remarked with satis-faction, rubbing his fingers testingly over the surface. "Hardly a lick this'll be needing."

Barley had smiled to herself, because she knew Dyke's licks. They took half a day and a thousand brush strokes. Dyke painting a signpost was in no more of a hurry than he was to breathe. He loved all of his work, but the paint-ing meant most to him, and always had.

"It's almost a piece of furniture," Hetty had once said admiringly, as Dyke put the finishing touches to the Fishpool to Makewith sign. He had been rather proud of this sign himself. Most of the posts were ordinary finger-posts pointing the roads, but whenever the name of a place took Dyke's fancy, it would bring out the artist in him, and he would fashion all kinds of curious devices.

Sometimes they took days, and he would wait eagerly for a wet spell when he could not paint or pace, and would sit for hours hunched over his carving.

At Fishpool one wet August he had made this beautiful curling waving fish with its tail flourishing towards the track with Makewith. Even Barley had agreed that it was a work of art, leaping there above the foxgloves and nettles, though on the whole she herself preferred the plain fingerposts. On wet days she liked to see Dyke carving a doll or toy for herself, and she fretted over the hours spent on posts that might just as well have been plain fingers.

Now Barley had reached the bottom of the hill and could hear her mother still singing. In the background as a kind of accompaniment was a busy scraping sound that Barley knew was the sound of a piece of rough bark being rubbed over the signpost to prepare it for painting tomorrow.

"Spring is come, Spring is here," carolled Hetty, who often made up tunes as she went along. Words, too, sometimes. "Birdies call and daisies peer."

It seemed a pity to disturb her. Besides, rubbing usually fetched the skin off Barley's knuckles, especially at the beginning of the season when they were still white and tender after the idle days of winter.

Barley looked round the encampment and admitted to herself that Hetty had made it very comfortable. Hetty treated each stopping place as if it were to be their home for ever, instead of just a few days, or even a single night. She was in her element making a home out of a few yards of turf and whatever materials came to hand.

"You've got a bit of the artist in you, for that matter,

Het," Dyke would often tell her, and Hetty never denied it.

Today, for instance, she *had* made use of the apronsful of wild flowers. They stood in cooking pans, jars, ewers—every container that was not in use, encircling the encampment with a ring of colour. Hetty had built a fireplace of stones in the centre, and the cauldron was already steaming. Barley sniffed. Rabbit! On the hot stones lay her favourite flat oaten cakes, nicely brown. Hetty had spread a cloth over the upturned box that served as a table, and set it out with flowers and napkins as if she were expecting the king himself to sup on her rabbit stew.

The tents were up in the shelter of the wagon, everything was ready.

"Barley!" Hetty, redfaced, looked up from her vigorous scrubbing. "Give the stew a stir, do. And give the oaties a turn, will you? Any signs?"

"Coming," replied Barley. "He'll be nearly here by now, I should think."

Obediently she took the long-handled spoon and stirred the pot, grateful to savour the rich brown smell of the juices.

"Dyke'll be able to start on the painting first thing," said Hetty with satisfaction, coming over to the fire. "Smooth as your elbow."

"Where will we go next?" asked Barley.

"One thing's certain," said Hetty, "it'll be on the way to Ingle. You know Dyke. It'll be six months since he last saw Pen."

Pen was Dyke's favourite brother. For that matter, he was Barley's favourite uncle. The Signposters visited him as often as they could in the summer. Luckily, Ingle was

*16*

right at the heart of Flockshire, the second biggest town, so with a little planning Dyke could make a visit half a dozen times in a season.

"Here he comes now," observed Hetty, and seizing the long-handled spoon she stirred the cauldron with a reckless vigour that showed how pleased she was. Barley ran to meet her father and held the reins as he dismounted.

"Rabbit!" he said, sniffing. "This place looks snug."

Hetty looked pleased and smoothed her apron.

"It'll do," she said. "Good pacing, Dyke?"

"Aye." But he would not stop to talk. He never would till he had loosened his dusty boots and plunged his face in water, and the three Signposters were sitting round the wooden box unfolding their napkins. Then, after a few smackings of the lips by way of a compliment to Hetty, he picked up his knife and fork and began eating and talking at the same time.

"I'll tell you what," he said, "I've said it a thousand times and I'll say it again. That Connery must've been a giant. Legs like steeples that man must've had."

"You have said so," agreed Hetty. "Many furlongs out, then?"

"Four!" said Dyke. "Twenty furlongs it says on the sign. Twenty-four furlongs I made it, and that striding out fit to stretch the legs clear off my body."

Hetty clucked her sympathy, but did not make too much of the matter. She knew that by the time the season was fairly under way, the same thing would have happened twenty times and would be a matter hardly worth remarking on.

Connery had been the Flockshire Signposter before Dyke had taken over, fifteen years ago. Now Dyke was a smallish man, though not for a minute did he think he was. "Middling tall and just the right man for the job," was how he described himself. Connery, on the other hand, had evidently been tall. And when it comes to pacing, long legs make long furlongs.

Two hundred and twenty paces to the furlong, was the rule. Dyke stuck to it as if it was a law made in heaven. He counted every step under his breath, and at the end of every furlong left a marker of twigs in the road. This was a safeguard, so that if he lost count later, he could come back to the sign and start recounting.

Not that Dyke was often known to lose count. It had only ever happened twice. Once was when he had suddenly rounded a corner and come upon a gallows with a dangling skein of bones. The other time was when a highwayman had held him up, thinking he might be rich. ("I had my best leather jerkin on that day, d'ye see," Dyke would explain apologetically.)

Hetty told a story how in the early days Dyke had gone off pacing leaving her to make supper. When he was not back by dusk she had set off to look for him. She had found him lying in a hole in the road where he had fallen and twisted his leg.

"Still counting!" she would cry. " 'One hundred and ninety-seven, one hundred and ninety-seven!' he kept saying. 'What's the matter, Dyke?' cried I. 'What's amiss?' 'One hundred and ninety-seven,' says he. 'Get a stick, Het, and write it in the dust.' And so I did, before he'd so much as say a word to me."

Hetty always enjoyed airing this story.

"What will you do about the difference, Dyke?" asked Hetty now. "You can't make twenty into twenty-four, try as you will. *Some*one's wrong."

"Someone is," agreed Dyke. "And if I can't match my steps to a giant, there's no blaming *me*."

"No one could match their steps to a giant, Dyke," said Hetty.

"Twenty-four full furlongs it is to Whipple, without a smidgeon of a doubt. It ain't a bit fair to put twenty, and then have poor ordinary mortals with mortal-size legs finding they've twenty-four to go."

"Ridiculous," agreed Hetty.

"But," said Dyke, spearing a succulent morsel of rabbit and softening his gaze, "I shall do as I always do. Split the difference."

Barley did a quick sum in her head.

"Twenty-*two* furlongs, father?" she said.

"Oh! The quickness!" exclaimed Hetty admiringly. She was made slightly dizzy by figures herself, and could never quite get over Dyke's own ability to count up to two hundred and twenty so many times in a day. There seemed to her to be just a hint of magic about it.

By now the light had almost faded. They sat wistfully wiping the last traces of gravy from their dishes with their crusts. The birds whistled in the greenish twilight and with a tingling of the spine Barley thought, "We're out again!" The wooden house and warm walls at Flock were suddenly a thousand miles away. A thin slice of moon curled above the wood and the beautiful icy smell of dew rushed up from the cooling earth. Barley could have cried aloud and thrown out her arms with joy. But the Signposters tried to keep calm at all times, it was part of their tradition. And at that moment, Barley wanted above anything else in the world to be a good Signposter. So she said nothing at all, and guessed that the others sat silent too for the very same reason.

# Chapter Two

Barley woke next morning huddled from a cold she had felt even while sleeping. She poked her head through the tent flap and blinked, dazzled by the fire of sun kindling acres of dew. She could hear it steadily dripping under the trees, heavily, as if dew were thicker than water.

A few drops ran down the tent and on to her warm bare neck. Barley shuddered deliciously and without stopping for thought stepped out and into the grass. She danced and ran and jumped. She had to. Her bare feet leaped from that snow-cold touch. She kicked up a fine spray and screamed as it stung her legs.

"Barley! Whatever? Barley!"

Hetty in her long flannel nightgown and frilled cap blinked astonished from the other tent.

Barley stopped. Straight away she felt cold. The wet hem of her nightgown flapped against her legs.

"You'll catch your death," said Hetty. "You give your legs a good rub and get some stockings on."

She was not nearly as angry as she might have been. Her eyes were wandering beyond Barley and her soaked nightdress to the glitter of the fields, and her nose twitched, suddenly surprised by freshness.

"Good day for painting," was all she said, and disappeared.

Barley dressed hurriedly and hung her blankets over the edge of the wagon as she had been taught.

"Never let the damp get in a blanket," Hetty warned. "Straight from the blanket to your bones, damp goes."

So Barley, who understood that damp bones were an unpleasant thing, always obeyed the rule.

Dyke came out of the tent already wearing his white apron so that he could start on the painting straight after breakfast. The morning evidently inspired him too.

"If you was to cast round in your mind a bit," he said thoughtfully, "you could think of something a bit unusual like for Straythorpe. You *could* . . ."

"No!" cried Barley and Hetty together.

He did not hear them.

"Straythorpe," he mused. "A plain finger seems a bit grudging for a name like that. Stray . . . Stray . . ."

Hetty and Barley exchanged glances. He was in danger of going right off into a trance and coming up with an inspiration that might keep them at Straythorpe for days on end.

"Good day, Signposters."

Barley and Hetty whirled round and Dyke was jerked from his dangerous dreaming. It was Quill, the pedlar, who had wintered in Flock in the same street as the Signposters. He went on foot, hump-backed from shouldering his bursting pack, his long thin nose pointing his way ahead.

"Quill!" exclaimed Hetty, gratefully watching Dyke come down to earth.

"We're off," he observed delightedly. "You and me, we're off again. Me peddling, you signpostering. Roads cross—I shall see you again."

He made to go. It was as if his legs could not wait for him.

"Where are you bound?" asked Dyke.

"Whipple, Plumtree, Makewith, Haze," chanted Quill. He was tiptoe to be off. "To Ingle before the end of the week."

"Ingle!" cried Dyke eagerly. "Ingle's where we're bound, isn't it, Hetty?"

She nodded. The Straythorpe post would remain a finger for this year, at least.

"Roads cross," nodded Quill again, and was away, with his curious smooth leaning walk, as if he were perpetually tumbling forwards and catching himself in time to take the next step.

"Ingle," said Dyke with satisfaction, sorting through his brushes. "It'll be good to see Family again."

Family, to Dyke, was everything, the mainspring of his life. It had even been the reason for his taking up sign-posting in the first place. He loved his Family with a steady, blind, unreasoning love. And the Flockshire Smiths were scattered through the shire as wide and far as if they had been seeded by a gale.

Barley knew from what Dyke and Hetty had told her that this was the fault of her great-grandfather, Dyke's grandfather Smith. She had heard the story a thousand times.

When grandfather Smith was forty he had been trampled by a horse he was shoeing and afterwards was never able to walk. He had always been a restless man, and to have to sit still was a very stern trial. Soon afterwards he had invented a rocking chair, because a chair that moved was at least better than a chair that stood with its four legs mulishly planted on the ground and not so much as a stir out of it. He would sit outside the door of his smithy, working himself feverishly to and fro, his bright eyes roving towards the rolling hills that lay beyond Flock, range upon tantalising range.

The invention of the rocking chair had made grandfather Smith very rich and famous. The smithy was turned into a workshop and Flock Rockers were turned out by the score. But even this did not satisfy him for very long. His eyes kept straying to the hills.

At last he hit upon a plan to cure his restlessness. He offered his sons a hundred guineas each to leave their native Flock and take to the road. In return, each Michaelmas Day, they were to visit him, and tell him the stories of their travels.

"Find your fortune," he told each in turn on his eighteenth birthday. Every one of them took up the challenge, for they were their father's sons. They took the hundred guineas and headed for the hills.

Even so, Dyke's problems would not have been so difficult if grandfather Smith's family had been a small one. But he had had eleven children, and only one of them a daughter.

Now, three generations later, the length and breadth of Flockshire was peopled with the wandering Smiths. The only consolation to Dyke was that the roaming instinct seemed to have died out, and his relatives all lived safely settled with roofs over their heads—with the exception of himself, that is. Grandfather Smith would have been proud of him. But Dyke himself would never admit to being a born wanderer.

"I do it because I have to," he would say obstinately. "*Someone's* got to keep the Family together."

Barley, who had seen her father staring sadly at the

white hills beyond Flock through the winter, and watched him counting the buds break as spring approached, did not believe him. This was partly because she felt exactly the same herself, and partly because she understood that Dyke enjoyed grumbling.

So it was that signposting and Family went hand in hand—it was impossible to tell where one ended and the other began. It sometimes seemed to Barley that she was related to the whole world. She had uncles, aunts, cousins, great-uncles, great-aunts and great-cousins in such numbers that she often needed a little prompting before she could remember their names. They were so spread out, and all so different from each other, that it was difficult to see them as a *family* at all. Barley sometimes tried to imagine them all standing crowded together under a gigantic umbrella. This picture made her giggle, but at least it helped her to see the Flockshire Smiths in a group that she could vaguely recognize as a Family.

"Better get started," remarked Hetty. "You get started, Dyke. Don't you fuss about the rest. Barley and me'll see to that."

The sooner Dyke was settled in to his work on a plain fingerpost, the happier she would be. Barley, who saw what she was after, offered eagerly:

"Here, father, I'll dry it down for you."

"I'll be giving the paint a stir," said Hetty.

Dyke looked at the pair of them and his usually far-away grey eyes were suddenly absolutely wide awake and absolutely seeing what was afoot.

Barley saw that he knew, but was not in the least afraid. Quill had spoken the word "Ingle" and Dyke had thought of Family. All was safe. But she knew that he knew, and reddened a little as she ran off to fetch the soft rags.

Dew dangled from the fingers of the post in long, dangerously balanced drops. If the post had not been set so firm by Dyke's capable hands, Barley could have given it a knock and watched them all go diving together to the grass below. As it was, she industriously wiped and rubbed until at the end she thought that it looked as good as new—hardly in need of paint at all. A lesser man than Dyke would have left it.

Afterwards she went to help Hetty at the encampment, which was a little way from the actual post. It always was. Dyke liked quiet while he worked. Barley had never so much as heard him whistle.

"Whistling is for peeling sticks," he would say. "It's for chopping wood and polishing brass, and the like. That's when it comes natural. But when a man's at work, really at work, he's too deep in things for whistling."

And so the Signposters worked contentedly through the morning, Dyke at his painting, Barley and Hetty at their tidying. And when the remains of the rabbit stew had been eaten, the fire put out and the embers scattered, they harnessed Cornish and took to the road for the second time that season. And they followed the white gleaming finger that pointed to Whipple, because Whipple led to Plumtree, and Plumtree to Makewith, Makewith to Haze, and Haze to a string of tiny hamlets, like beads on the long thread of the road that led at last to Ingle. And Ingle was Family.

# Chapter Three

It was just a week later when the Signposters came to Ingle. Dyke, having painted eleven signposts and carried out five pacings, and being lit by the prospect of seeing Family at last, could not contain himself. He found it impossible to sit on the wagon behind the dawdling Cornish, and jumped down and walked the last five miles, as if he thought his own legs would take him there more quickly. Barley, caught by the same mood of impatience, jumped down and kept him company, leaving Hetty up there to hold the reins and badger Cornish.

The approach to Ingle was down a steep hill, and they came at last to it at evening, at sudden cold dewfall. They paused at the top, as they always did, taking in the sights of the town below them.

"Look!" cried Barley. "The church!"

"Lawk!" cried Hetty. "How it's growed! Look at that steeple! Hasn't it *growed*?"

Dyke was irritated by Hetty's talking as though the church had pushed up a steeple all by itself as if it were a daffodil bulb sprouting. His brother Pen was master builder at Ingle, a true craftsman, and entitled to his credit.

"Steeples don't *grow*," he pointed out. "They get

*builded.* And what's more, steeples is tricky. But Pen's not the man to put up a tower because he's afraid of a steeple."

He stared down with pride to where the church stood, on the outskirts of the little town. The stones glowed in the last fires of sunset, and the lines rose clean and true from the green turf. It was beautiful. In fact, what with one thing and another, Dyke found himself having to swallow hard.

"Come on," he said gruffly. "Pen'll be waiting supper."

Pen already knew that they were coming. He always left a homing pigeon at Haze at the beginning of the season. Barley had run straight to its loft and flung up the shutter, and all three of them had watched it turn to a speck and disappear.

"That'll make sure of our supper tomorrow night," Dyke had said with satisfaction.

Barley was thinking of her supper now as she began to race down the hill, leaving Hetty and Dyke to follow more sedately. However much they might lark in private, they liked to appear as dignified as possible in public, mindful of the Signposter tradition. Hetty, in any case, was wearing her best clothes, and she never hurried in *them.*

Uncle Pen's house was only a stone's throw from the new church. He had built it himself, and he and his apprentice masons had built the garden. It was full of the stone figures they carved and chiselled in their spare time—if a stonemason can ever be said to have spare time. Neither Pen nor any of his men could leave a piece of stone alone.

"We've got stones in the blood," he would say with pride.

This remark used to worry Barley when she was

27

younger, but as year followed year and neither Pen nor any of the apprentices showed signs of turning into statues themselves, she gradually became reassured.

It was still a relief, though, when advancing through the array of stone griffins, lions, bears and cocks, she saw the unmistakably live figure of Uncle Pen himself. She had a brief glimpse of his red face and round shiny pate fringed with sandy hair, and then she was muffled against his canvas apron, its rough hair scratching her cheek, and full of the familiar smell of wood and plaster.

"Here she is!" cried Uncle Pen, delighted. "My little maid from Flock. And haven't you growed?"

"Not so much as your steeple," said Barley. "It's beautiful, Uncle Pen."

"Up in the sky, where it should be," remarked Uncle Pen with satisfaction.

Then Hetty and Dyke were there, and Hetty knocked her bonnet askew embracing Uncle Pen, and Dyke, who had been bursting with news to tell all the way from Flock, just stood there, wordless and beaming like a candle.

Hetty, excited as she was, was by no means struck dumb. She gabbled on about the state of the roads between Haze and Ingle, and remarked on the new thatch Pen had given his house.

"It was getting a bit thin," she said. "Houses is like menfolk—all the better for a good head of hair."

Which some men with bald pates and fringes might have taken as rude and meaningful, but Pen just stood there smiling and nodding at every single word that Hetty said. She was about to start on again about the steeple growing, but caught Dyke's eye, and said instead:

"What a deal of *building* that steeple must have taken, Pen. I love a steeple. Them towers they never seem to *get* anywhere. just stopping lopped off short in mid air. But a steeple—ah, a steeple's lovely. There's some *point* to a steeple. It *gets* somewhere."

Both Pen and Dyke nodded approvingly at this speech, and Hetty straightened her bonnet and looked at Dyke as if to say, "There, now, I *can* make sensible remarks about steeples, for all your criticizing."

"Supper now, then?" suggested Uncle Pen.

"I'll get Cornish seen to," said Dyke.

"And me'n' Barley'll give you a hand, Pen," said Hetty.

They went among the statues to the cottage. As she stepped inside, Barley had the usual feeling of being home at last. Their own house in Flock never seemed so much a real home as Uncle Pen's. Perhaps this was because the Flock house was only lived in for half the year, and knew it was only second best for the Signposters. At any rate, it always seemed to Barley to be drawn up stiff in an offended kind of way. The difference might also be due to the fact that Uncle Pen had no wife, and there was no best parlour, with the kind of furniture that seemed to dare you to use it. He lived as snug as a fox in its den in one big, whitewashed room with a low beamy ceiling and stone floor littered with mats.

Even Hetty, who was a great one for going round plumping up cushions and clucking over pieces of fluff, let him alone. Now she pulled the strings of her bonnet and hung it on the hook on the back door next to Uncle Pen's jerkin without so much as rubbing her finger over it first for dust.

Pen was turning a chicken on the spit. He always cooked chicken for supper on the first night of the Signposters' new season, with Christmas pudding to follow, stuffed to blackness with fruit.

"It's as good as Christmas, you coming," he would say, "and deserves as good to eat."

He didn't put holly on the pudding, but he did pour brandy over it and set fire to it, and the sense of occasion when the thin blue flames floated above it, veiling Uncle Pen's excited face, was enormous. Afterwards they sat round the fire with sweetmeats, roasting their toes and now and then a shovel of chestnuts.

This supper seemed to Barley to have been even better than ever, and as she sank into a large Flock Rocker by the ingle nook, she knew she would have to be very careful. Hetty was very quick at detecting a nod or yawn, however cleverly disguised, and would pack Barley off to her cupboard bed at the first suspicion of either.

There they sat, the flames lighting their faces, quite ridiculously happy and content, not merely because the chicken had been juicy and the pudding smothered in a new cinnamon sauce of Pen's invention, but simply because they were Family again. There had to be at least four of the Flockshire Smiths gathered in one place for Dyke, at any rate, to feel one of a Family.

"How's the carving, then, Pen?" asked Dyke at last. "Coming nicely?"

"Nicely, thank you, Dyke," he returned. "I'm on an acorn frieze now. Just did my seventy-fourth this afternoon. Getting the feel of acorns now."

"My word," said Hetty. "You must be. All them!"

They all sat and contemplated the thought of seventy-four acorns growing out of stone, and more to come.

"I've got the letters ready, Dyke," remarked Uncle Pen, folding his hands over his stomach, and creaking his Flock Rocker.

"Ah," returned Dyke. "You would have, Pen. Never known you fail."

"One for everybody, Pen?" asked Hetty, knowing the answer already.

"Every one, Het."

"And how many's that?" asked Dyke. "One hundred and twenty-six, do you reckon?"

"Seven," amended Pen. "You'd perhaps be forgetting Kit."

"One hundred and twenty-seven!" cried Hetty ecstatically. "And that's not counting the babies, bless their hearts! I don't know how you do it, Pen."

"I've got all winter," said Pen. "And I'm fond of writing, as you know. A letter for every Smith in Flockshire, and not two of 'em the same!"

"Fancy!" Hetty was overcome. "Just fancy!"

Every year it was the same. Uncle Pen had a sack of letters waiting for the Signposters to collect and deliver on their rounds of the Flockshire Smiths. He had two scrolls filled with their names and addresses. He was almost as Family-minded as Dyke himself.

"What you should do, Pen," observed Dyke, "is shut up shop, let the steeple take care of itself, and come along with us."

"Now, Dyke," said Pen, "you know the answer to that one."

"Haven't you got just a bit of an urge to travel, then?" asked Hetty. "Not just a bit?"

"Listen," said Uncle Pen. "There's folks like you, and there's folks like me. My toes is like roots. And you know what happens to a tree when the roots comes up."

Dyke and Hetty nodded gravely. Put like that, it seemed dangerous to push the matter further. Barley looked curiously at Uncle Pen's feet and observed that toes like roots seemed to fit into ordinary shoes much the same as everyone else's.

"Besides," Uncle Pen went on, "this year there's the fair."

"Fair, Pen?" prompted Dyke.

"Michaelmas Fair," said Pen. "And that church must be ready."

"Of course!" Dyke slapped his knee. "We'd clear forgotten, Het! The Michaelmas Fair. I was only a bit of a lad last time it was at Ingle. Oh my!"

Barley knew from what Hetty and Dyke had told her that the annual Michaelmas Fair, usually held in Flock, was held at Ingle once every twenty-five years. This was in honour of a man who had once lived there and saved his lord's life in battle.

Hetty sat slowly shaking her head.

"Michaelmas," she said. "If ever that word's spoke, your grandfather Smith comes straight to my mind, Dyke."

"Aye," agreed Pen. "That was the day for him. Every Smith in Flockshire was on his doorstep that day of the year."

"Just fancy," went on Hetty, "if he was alive today.

33

One hundred and twenty-seven Smiths all together at one time. *Wouldn't he have blinked?*"

"Ah!" sighed Pen. "Those days will never come again. Wouldn't it be *beautiful*? The whole Family, all brought together. Beautiful."

He sighed again. They sat there, all four of them, looking into the flames. And as they sat there, the silence suddenly came alive, it grew and thickened and roared in their ears. And if all of them knew it, and all of them half knew what it was trying to say to them, it was Dyke who finally, trembling and suddenly gone very pale, cried out:

"Oh! Oh! It must be! The Family! We've hit on it at last! Oh! Oh! The Family!"

And Barley, seeing her father's blind white face, and because she had never before seen a dream born before her very eyes, burst into tears.

# Chapter Four

Next morning the Signposters bravely looked at their dream in the cold light of day. Barley, waking in her dark cupboard bed, lay there, listening to Pen clattering pails and raking the fire, and in her mind went over what had happened the night before.

They had sat there till midnight, Hetty in her excitement blinded to Barley's jaw-splitting yawns and drooping lids.

"It can be done!" Dyke had kept declaring. Over and over again he said it, as if the words themselves had some peculiar magic and the mere saying of them turned impossibilities into certainties.

Uncle Pen, who was of a less impulsive nature, once he had got over the first excitement, began finding obstacles despite himself.

"It's a beautiful *idea*," he said, "that I don't deny. But the numbers, Dyke. That's the splinter in the stew. I don't say we can't get *some* of 'em here for Michaelmas."

But you could no more damp Dyke than you could put out a star with a pitcher of water.

"*All* of them!" he cried. "Every Smith in Flockshire! Think of it—the whole Family together at last! Just once. Just once in a lifetime."

Hetty, who had had to keep dabbing at her eyes with the corner of her shawl, downright sobbed at this. She had always been proud of having married into the Flockshire Smiths. She herself came of a very small family. Her only living relative was a deaf aunt in Firbeck. After her only son Henry had run away from home over twenty years ago (thus depriving Hetty of another relative) the poor lady had become a little muddled in the head. She kept mistaking Hetty for somebody else and calling her "Lettice", so it was difficult for her to work up any Family Feeling of her own.

Barley, forgotten in her corner, conjured up her own private picture of the gigantic umbrella. The Flockshire Smiths crowded beneath it stared solemnly back at her, as they always did. And then, all of a sudden, the trick worked. She *saw* them as a family. Suddenly they all belonged there, crouched and squeezed awkwardly together, and their faces blurred into a pale smudge. Barley's own eyes were watering again, and, once and for all, she was on her father's side.

"We must, we must!" she heard herself saying, and Dyke nodded at her and said, "That's my lass," and Pen cracked open a nut to hide his emotion.

Barley slid open a door of her bed and found to her surprise that the big room looked exactly the same as it had done yesterday. She had half-expected it to be different, as if after last night nothing could ever be quite the same again. Hetty came in wearing her ordinary brown stuff dress, which Barley immediately knew as a sign that they would be moving on today.

"Come along and get washed," said Hetty. "Your father wants an early start."

Water cold from the pump made Barley wide awake

*36*

in an instant. Hetty was banging about with pots and pans, getting the breakfast.

"Where's Uncle Pen?" asked Barley.

"Church," said Hetty briefly. "Doing another acorn."

"Oh."

"He likes to get an acorn done before breakfast. Says it starts the day off right. Now, where's that dratted dripping?"

Barley dressed and wandered out into the garden. Birds whistled, cocks crowed, and Uncle Pen chipped at his acorn. Dyke was there, sitting on a stone wolf, his gaiters soaking in the grass. Barley saw that he was engaged in "catching his death" while Hetty wasn't looking. She could tell at a glance that wet grass and a grey mist had done nothing to damp his fire. He would never let go now. She had to call several times before he heard her.

"Where are we going, father?" she asked. "We *are* going today, aren't we?"

Dyke nodded.

"To Wick's," he told her. "Wick first, and then on to the Lamfrey Makers."

"Do you really think they'll all come?" asked Barley.

"Every one of 'em," said Dyke with finality. He slapped his hand hard on the stone wolf's head and almost at the same moment the sun broke through the mist.

Straight after breakfast the Signposters left Ingle. Uncle Pen climbed up and sat on the roof of the church so that he could see them out of sight.

The sack of letters was put on the wagon, together with a pork pie and a stone jar of elderberry wine, and they were off. Barley kept craning behind to see Uncle Pen's energetic figure.

"It's dangerous to stand on roofs waving," said Hetty.

"You'd think folks'd have more sense."

But she turned back and waved several times herself, and her handkerchief kept travelling up to her eyes.

It seemed to Barley, as at last they cleared the brow of the hill and left Ingle behind, that the road had never stretched so beckoningly before them. Never had Flockshire seemed so excitingly crammed with Smiths and signposts. Every season she could ever remember had been exciting in its own way, but this year was going to be better than ever, because it had a purpose. She saw the summer stretching ahead like a hill, with Michaelmas Day and the Family reunion glittering at the summit.

It was only a day's journey to Uncle Wick's if you kept going, without stopping to pace or paint. Dyke had no patience for either today. Straight to Wick's they galloped. They travelled, at least, as fast as Cornish was willing, which was rather short of a gallop.

The Signposters' high spirits, which showed themselves early in the day by loud singing and rollicking choruses, were beginning to flag by the time they approached Bilbury. For one thing, the weather was changing. The sun went in, a cold wind blew up, and the countryside looked suddenly bleak and unspringlike. It was growing dark, the night hastened by the inky clouds rolling in to fill the sky.

"I'm not sure but what we're doing the wrong thing, Dyke," Hetty offered at last, after a silence that had lasted a full two miles. Her voice was gloomy. She was very much affected by the weather. If Barley wanted to ask a favour, she always waited for a sunny day to do it.

Neither Dyke nor Barley replied. They were too sunk in silence to rouse themselves out of it all in a minute.

After a few more minutes, Hetty heaved a sigh, a vast, graveyard sigh.

"The more I think," she said, "the more I'm sure."

"Sure what, Hetty?" asked Dyke absently.

"But what we're doing the wrong thing. Wick's not the man for reunions, Dyke."

Dyke merely grunted. Barley could not help fearing that her mother was right. Of all her uncles, she liked Uncle Wick least. He was a stout, wheezing man, whose eyes were tiny and poking and who always gave his opinions as if they wre not so much opinions as laws. He was a candle-maker by trade, and Barley always thought his candles gave him away more than anything else. If Uncle Pen had been making them, they would have been like his stones—made joyfully into shapes and figures with twists and twirls and impossible spirals. But Uncle Wick's candles were every one the same, except that some were short and fat and dull and others were long and thin and dull. Barley felt that if just *sometimes* he could stretch to a few twirls she might be able to like him better.

"Apart from which," went on Hetty, who having once settled into gloom was bent on nothing short of tragedy, "I can't help feeling but what it's a bit tactless."

"Tactless?" said Dyke.

"On account of *Kit*." Hetty spoke with awful emphasis. "Reunions isn't a thing to bring up with a man whose own son's run off from home."

"Aye," agreed Dyke, "but that was last year, Hetty. They'll be over it by now."

"Over it!" snorted Hetty. "You don't get over your own flesh and blood running off into the night with not so much as a word or sign or whisper of warning. Over it! Mathilda was bawling when we went by in April, and was still at it in September, as I remember. Wick said she'd never stopped. Not once."

Barley secretly did not blame Kit at all for running away. Neither Uncle Wick nor Aunt Mathilda seemed any reason for staying. And a lifetime of making candles certainly did not. Barley knew that that, really, was why he had gone. Uncle Wick had always taken it for granted that Kit would follow in his footsteps. But Kit was quick and always alive with laughter, Barley's favourite cousin. He was not cut out for candles, even she could see that.

"Wick's as much for Family as I am," said Dyke obstinately. A bit of an argument always made him obstinate. Even if he knew in his heart that Hetty was right, he would never admit it now.

"Now you know that's not true, Dyke Signposter," retorted Hetty. "Not a day's ride from Pen does he live, and not one visit has he paid for ten year and more."

"He's not comfortable on a horse," said Dyke with dignity.

Barley, conjuring up Uncle Wick's enormous girth, reflected that the horse probably wasn't very comfortable, either.

Hetty did not reply. In the distance there were lights nuzzling the gloom. They were there! Barley gave a little shiver. It was not just because the wind was blowing up her cloak and letting in floods of cold air against her warm skin. It was because Dyke's dream was about to be put to the test. And it seemed to Barley that Uncle Wick was test enough for any dream.

# Chapter Five

Uncle Wick's house was made of wood and leaning against it was his workroom and shop. The Signposters saw at once that he was in, because a lighted candle flickered in the window.

"Ah," said Dyke with satisfaction, throwing off the dark mood that had settled on him during the last part of the journey. "Wick's home. And we're about right for supper, I should guess."

"They're not expecting us," warned Hetty. "So don't go expecting too much. And if I was you, I should wait till morning to mention that little matter we was talking of."

Dyke's independence flared up again.

"I shall do no such thing, Hetty," he cried warmly. "Wick's my own flesh and blood, and I don't have to be mealy-mouthed with *him*, I hope."

"Of course not, Dyke," said Hetty soothingly. "I was just thinking—"

"Well, don't," said Dyke.

So Hetty didn't—not out loud, at any rate. But Barley could tell by the way she slammed the bags out of the wagon that a good deal of explosive thinking was going on inside her head.

"Give a knock at the door, Barley," she said. "We shall catch our deaths in this wind."

But there was no need. A blurred face appeared behind the candle like a jack o' lantern. Next minute it vanished again and there was a loud rattling of bolts and keys. Uncle Wick had a great dread of burglars. Hetty often said that if she had a pair of shoes for every lock and bolt on his doors and windows, she would be shod for life.

The door opened. There was a shriek from inside the house and all the candles blew out.

"Wick! Wick!" came Aunt Mathilda's anguished wail. "I can't see! What's amiss? Oh Wick, come to me!"

"Drat," said Uncle Wick, by way of a greeting to the weary Signposters. "There's not a candle in the house left lit."

"It's the wind, Wick," said Dyke apologetically. Barley often wished he would stand up more to Uncle Wick. She supposed it was because Dyke was the younger of the two and couldn't get out of the habit of looking up to him.

"Eh?" came Uncle Wick's voice. "Dyke? Is that you, Dyke?"

"It's all of us!" cried Dyke joyfully. "Let's all get inside with the door shut and see about lighting the candles."

"Come on, then," said Uncle Wick. They could just make out his bulbous, shadowy shape. "There'll be no candles lit while this wind's blowing straight through the house as if it owned it."

He sounded annoyed. Barley could tell that he blamed the Signposters for the weather. They trooped inside, pressing together in the narrow passage while Uncle Wick slammed the door behind them and began to shoot

*42*

back the bolts. At the end of the passage a candle appeared and behind it the startled face of Aunt Mathilda.

"Lawks and gracious!" she exclaimed. "You!"

"Us, Mathilda," agreed Dyke. "And how have you fared this winter?"

"It's a funny time of the day to arrive," she said. "At *night*."

"Not really night, now, Mathilda," said Dyke.

"Dark," said Aunt Mathilda, "and dark's night, so far as *I* know anything."

"Oh dear," Barley heard her mother say under her breath, "we *have* caught them wrong."

"You'd best come along in, I suppose," said Aunt Mathilda, and led the way into the living room.

"Ah," said Dyke, determined not to be put off, "now we can see what's what."

This was only just true. In fact, Wick's living room was always darker than any other Barley knew. Being a candle-maker did not seem to go hand in hand with a fondness for light and flicker. A bare four candles and a handful of fire hiding at the back of the chimney set a cheerless scene that was not at all what the end of a journey should be. Barley's first quick scan showed her not a sign of supper and she thought of Uncle Pen and his turning chicken and eager, bustling welcome. "There's family," she thought, "and there's *family*."

"Well then, Wick, well then, Mathilda," said Dyke, with absolute determination to stir up some glow of Family Feeling. "This is a treat."

Uncle Wick and Aunt Mathilda neither agreed nor disagreed. They did not even hear what he said. One was still at the door, banging bolts as if he could hear burglars galloping in the street outside. The other had disappeared altogether, up the ladder that led to the bedrooms. Barley could see that Hetty was trying hard to catch Dyke's eye so that she could make a face that meant "I told you so." But Dyke carefully avoided looking at her and strolled about the room humming as if he saw nothing at all untoward in their welcome.

"Well, then!" exclaimed Aunt Mathilda, reappearing down the ladder. "You did give us a turn. Wick, do stop banging those bolts. You'd better take your things off and get to the fire. Oh *Wick*!"

Aunt Mathilda seemed slightly better humoured since her disappearance into the bedroom. The reason for this, as Barley could quite easily see, was a change of shawl. The one she now wore was the one she always wore when the Signposters arrived as expected visitors, and was evidently her best. It was of yellow wool painstakingly embroidered with woolly rosebuds and was altogether very surprising considering Aunt Mathilda.

The Signposters obediently removed their things, and Dyke produced Pen's letter, which Mathilda took and propped on the table without the least eagerness to open it. Uncle Wick, his bolts thoroughly shot, joined them, and soon they found themselves sitting round the chimney where the fire was either dead or pretending to be. Barley took another look around the room, but could see no sign of a meal either recently eaten or in preparation, and her heart sank. Aunt Mathilda sat with the rest of them and showed not a sign of beginning to bustle round with pots and pans. Barley's fingers were stiff and cold after the long drive and she longed to hold them to a flame. She was hungry, too. "I could eat a rabbit," she thought. "A whole rabbit, all to myself."

Uncle Wick struck up.

"*This* is unexpected, Dyke and Henrietta," he said. He would insist on calling Hetty by her full name, more for his own dignity's sake than hers. This would not have mattered so much, Barley thought, except that Hetty, as soon as she was addressed as Henrietta, felt called upon to *act* like a Henrietta. And this made her so spiky and stiff and correct, and so unlike the real careless, happy person who went under the name of Hetty, that Barley felt positively ill at ease with her.

"Usually, of course," went on Uncle Wick, "you are not with us for another week. Possibly more. Yes. Possibly more. Possibly."

"Possibly," agreed poor Hetty, so flummoxed that her voice came out exactly the same as Uncle Wick's.

Barley stared at her.

"*Possibly*," said Uncle Wick again, giving Hetty a sharp look. She went very red and began to look wildly around the room as if at all costs to avoid his eyes and change the subject.

"Oh Mathilda!" she half-shrieked. "*What* a good idea to turn the room round. I *knew* the minute I set foot that something was different. That table *never* used to be next that potholder, and I'll *swear* that chair you're sitting on was next to the ladder, as sure as I'm alive!"

Her outburst caused Uncle Wick to drum his heels and puff his cheeks. Aunt Mathilda, on the other hand, was charmed.

"Fancy you noticing, Henrietta," she cried. "And do you like it?"

"Oh I do!" cried Hetty fervently. "I *do*!"

Aunt Mathilda's delight coloured her whole face pink, with particular emphasis on the pointed tip of her nose.

"Well," she said, "and so do I. But fancy you noticing." She paused. "Now then, what about a bite of supper?"

"Oh yes, please!" cried Barley, and clapped a hand to her mouth as Hetty turned to frown.

"Well, Mathilda," she replied, "I don't think any of us will say no. But don't go to a lot of bother and fuss. A bit of bread and cheese will do us nicely."

"Oh no, no," replied Aunt Mathilda grandly. The wearing of the rosebud shawl and Hetty's admiration of her furnishing had evidently brought out the hostess in her. "There's a stew only wants hotting up. And I've a loaf made fresh this morning to dip into it. And I've a fancy for some ginger pudding and custard."

As she rose and went out into the kitchen Barley came very close to liking her.

"I'll give you a hand, Mathilda," said Hetty, and went after her.

Barley often thought afterwards that this was the real reason for the dreadful scene that followed. If only Hetty had sat on by the fire, able to pull faces at Dyke and dig him with her elbow, none of it would ever have happened. And what *did* happen, Barley could never remember afterwards without coming out in gooseflesh and shutting her eyes, tight.

# Chapter Six

Pots began to bang in the kitchen and at the same time a few flames came darting up from the back of the chimney. Outside the wind howled and there was a sudden flurry of rain on the window.

"Sounds like hail," observed Dyke comfortably, edging his chair nearer the fire.

"You're early this year, Dyke," said Uncle Wick for the second time. "Haven't you seen Pen?"

"Oh yes," said Dyke excitedly, seeing his opening. "In fact, that's why I've been in such a rush to get to you, Wick."

Uncle Wick looked long and hard at Dyke.

"Explain yourself," he said.

"It's an idea I had," began Dyke, his face beginning to come alight. "At least, an idea we all had, in a manner of speaking. All of us had it, really. It's to do with Family, Wick. You know—the sort of idea that just won't wait, that keeps pushing you along with it as if you couldn't help yourself. *You* know the sort of idea."

Uncle Wick neither spoke, nor nodded, nor shook his head. He just sat there waiting for Dyke to go on, and Barley, watching them both, felt quite certain that Uncle Wick had never had an idea of the sort in his whole life. If he had, it would have showed in his candles.

Dyke, not noticing Uncle Wick's silence and sternness, rushed on.

"The idea," he said joyfully, never for a moment doubting the delight he was about to give, "is for a reunion!"

He waited. The wind rattled the bolts and chains and moaned in the chimney, sending a gust of smoke into the room that set Uncle Wick spluttering and coughing and wheezing till Dyke had to drum him on the back to cure him.

"A-a-shoo!" wheezed Uncle Wick. "A-a-what?"

"A reunion!" cried Dyke. "A *Family* reunion!"

Uncle Wick's cough stopped suddenly and miraculously.

"Family reunion?" he repeated. "Explain yourself."

So Dyke explained himself. He explained how the Michaelmas Fair was to be held at Ingle, and how that had put him in mind of grandfather Smith and his yearly reunions.

"And we can have one again!" he cried. "Every Smith from every corner of Flockshire. The whole Family, Wick, from A to Z, from great-grandfathers to—"

"*Stop!*" thundered Uncle Wick.

Dyke stopped. So did the clattering and chattering in the kitchen. Barley, rigid in her Flock Rocker, saw Aunt Mathilda and Hetty come rushing out from the kitchen, wiping their hands on their pinafores. Hetty, with a quick glance at Dyke's open-mouthed surprise and Wick's furious face and pointing forefinger, guessed at once what had happened.

"Oh Dyke!" she cried. "What *have* you been going

and saying? After all I said to you on the way here! What *have* you—?"

"Silence!" roared Uncle Wick, wheeling in his chair so that the pointing finger was now directed towards Hetty herself. "I won't have it! I won't!"

"Oh Wick!" moaned Aunt Mathilda. "Wick!"

She threw up her arms in a gesture so sweeping that she flung the rosebud shawl off her shoulders and on to the floor without so much as a sign that she had even noticed it.

"What's amiss, Wick?" she cried. "Tell us, tell us!"

"Let him tell you," said Uncle Wick, bringing the finger back to poor Dyke, who seemed unable to say a word. Luckily, Uncle Wick did not intend him to. "Let *him* tell you. My own brother, who comes into my house and sits by my fire and turns on me like a ravening wolf!"

Aunt Mathilda let out a little squeal and Hetty said sharply, "Now come along, Wick. There's no call for that kind of talk."

"Have you," demanded Uncle Wick, "since setting foot in this house, have you so much as asked after, or mentioned, or hinted at mentioning or asking after—our son?"

There was a very long silence. Barley shut her eyes and thought of Kit.

"Now come along, Wick," said Dyke. His voice came easily now with the pity he felt. "Don't take it hard. It wasn't meant like that. We didn't like to bring the matter up, Wick, and that's all there is to it. Poor Mathilda's had enough to bear this last year, with Kit running off and—"

"*What?*" Wick's voice bent the candle-flames and set the shadows into a wild scurry. "*What* did you say?"

"I said—well—about Kit running off—" stammered the bewildered Dyke.

"Oooooeaoooh!" Aunt Mathilda uttered a long rising wail and began to pull the pins out of her hair and toss them about her in a sharp shower. Barley, watching her, could tell that this was a very bad sign.

"There now!" Uncle Wick pushed back his chair and stood up, towering over Dyke. "See what you've done now. You've set her off again."

"I-I-I—" began Dyke.

"He's done nothing of the kind," snapped Hetty. She herself might blame Dyke for the whole scene, but she knew where her loyalty lay. "All he did was tell you about the idea he's had. And a very good idea it is, too. And any intention of hurting anybody's feelings is right out of the question. *You* know Dyke better than that. Now hush up, Mathilda, do. And pick those pins up, Barley, and give them to your aunt."

To Barley, crawling on the flagstones on her hands and knees searching for pins that were still raining past her as she worked, the rest of the scene was a blur of high, angry voices, of swishing skirts and stamping feet.

"He did *not* run away," she heard Aunt Mathilda wail. "The idea! The idea! As if our precious Kit would do such a thing. He *didn't* run away!"

"Didn't he?" asked Hetty. "What did happen, then?"

"He was stolen," cried Aunt Mathilda passionately. "He was stolen by the gypsies!"

"Stolen?" Hetty's voice was high and incredulous. "By the gypsies? A great big lad like that? Oh Mathilda, you don't believe *that*!"

"I do, I do, I *do*!" squealed Aunt Mathilda.

Barley, raising her head and sniffing, detected a faint smell of burning and remembered the stew.

"I think something's burning," she ventured in a small voice. She might as well have been a cricket on the hearth for all the notice they took of her.

"We *both* do!" roared Uncle Wick. "*Now!*"

"Well, then," said Dyke placatingly, "perhaps he might have been, at that."

"Rubbish!" snorted Hetty. Her skirts swirled in front of Barley's nose. Now that she was roused, the battle was hers, not Dyke's. "Stolen by the gypsies indeed! I'm sorry for you both, downright sorry, as I would be for myself if any child of mine upped and left me without so much as a word. But as for putting it on the gypsies, it's right out of reason, and I'm bound to say so, if I hang for it. I never—"

"Now, Hetty, now—" Dyke's gaitered legs hurried across and Barley knelt upright in time to see Uncle Wick, legs astride, point a last, terrible finger and cry "*Go!*"

It was suddenly so quiet that Barley could hardly believe that no one but herself noticed the smell of burning stew. Then Hetty twitched her skirt, took Dyke's arm and swirled towards the door, sweeping her bonnet and shawl off the back of a chair as she went. Barley dropped her handful of pins, scrambled to her feet, snatched up her own things and ran down the passage after them. At the front door Hetty turned.

"And as for Family Feeling," she said, very clearly and distinctly, "pish!"

She turned and pulled at the knob with a final toss of the head, ready to leave a gape-mouthed Uncle Wick and hair-pulling Aunt Mathilda as she swept out into the night. Nothing happened.

"The bolts, Dyke. The bolts!" hissed Hetty, keeping her head high.

Dyke bent and fumbled with the chains. His fingers bodged and struggled with the massive bolts. One, two, three . . . Barley closed her eyes again to shut out the awful picture, and after what seemed like hours the last key was turned, the door opened and the wind blew in. The Signposters stumbled out into the dark and wet, followed by the smell of ginger pudding and burning stew, and a last shriek from Aunt Mathilda as all the candles blew out again.

An hour later the Signposters finally pitched camp a mile outside Bilbury. Hetty had wanted to knock up the seamstress in the village, who was a friend of hers, but Dyke was adamant.

"It would shame the Family," he said firmly. "This is between Wick and me. It's a Family matter, and we don't want all Flockshire to know of it."

Hetty had realized it was useless to argue, and they had driven out of Bilbury, the rain beating on their faces in a night as black as ink.

Now they sat huddled and bedraggled under the canvas hoop of the wagon, cramped up among the paints and pans and posts. Dyke had lit a storm lantern so that Hetty could search round for some food and blankets.

"I knew it would happen," said Hetty at last, pushing down the last bite of bread and cheese without any butter. Her face peered mournfully above her blanket. Water ran off the edge of her bonnet and the lantern shone on her wet cheeks.

"And there would have been rabbit stew," said Barley. "It smelled so good before it began to burn."

"Burn?" said Hetty sharply.

"Yes," said Barley. "Didn't you smell it?"

But Hetty was laughing. She didn't seem able to help herself. She didn't laugh out loud, but in a gasping, painful sort of way, almost as if it hurt her. Dyke and Barley stared at her until at last she stopped as abruptly as she had begun.

In the silence the cold and wet gathered about them. Rain, sharp as hail, splattered on the canvas, and the sharp ice of the wind rushed in and cut about them. Barley moved closer to Hetty, longing for warmth, and Hetty put an arm round her, understanding. Dyke cleared his throat.

"If you have an idea," he said doggedly at last, "you have to stick by it. I'm not saying that some ginger pudding wouldn't have been very warming. I'm sorry about that, Barley and Het, as you know I am. But you can't bottle up a dream, not for the sake of a Wick."

Just then the storm lantern went out and left the Signposters staring into the darkness while Dyke's words sank in. And despite everything, they all fell asleep believing what he said.

# Chapter Seven

The Signposters were very stiff next morning. Dyke, in particular, kept rubbing his back and hobbled about as bent as Quill himself.

"Humph!" sniffed Hetty. "It's one thing to have Family feeling and another to let your bones go to rack and ruin. But I shan't say any more about it."

Nor did she. Barley knew that her mother was really on Dyke's side, despite the way she carried on grumbling about the state of her clothes after being slept in, and the muddiness of the road about them. Her good humour was finally and fully restored when on removing her cloak she found she was still wearing the pinafore Aunt Mathilda had lent her the night before. She looked so odd in it, still in her bonnet with the embroidered pinafore trailing in the long wet grass, that all the Signposters were set laughing. After that, the scene of the night before seemed not so dreadful after all, and as they ate their breakfast they cheerfully planned where they would go next.

"The Lamfrey Makers," said Dyke with decision.

"Oh *yes*!" cried Hetty and Barley together.

Hetty enjoyed going to Lamfrey because it was a real town with shops and two markets every week. Besides, her remaining relative lived in nearby Firbeck (even if she did call Hetty Lettice) and she herself had spent her girlhood in the next village. Hetty talked very hard all the time she was in Lamfrey.

Barley liked going chiefly because of the Makers themselves. They were her favourite branch of the Flockshire Smiths—after Uncle Pen, of course. They were exactly what their names said they were—Makers. There were about twenty of them, all different—some dreamy, some noisy, some sad and some gay, but all Makers to their marrow.

"We don't care what we make," was their motto. "It's the making that counts."

You had only to look into the window of their shop to see that that was true. They could turn their hand to anything, as the fancy took them. They made pictures, chairs, dresses, jugs, ropes, beads, cushions, mats, weathercocks, birdcages and painted mottoes. Last year some of them had been going through a spell of making straw hats for the haymakers and their horses.

"What will it be this year?" she wondered out loud.

"Makers will always think of something," replied Dyke.

He finished harnessing Cornish and soon they were away and shaking off memories of the night before. To help them, the sun came out, and flashed over the soaked trees and grass with such sudden and startling beauty that Dyke was moved to remark, "If there wasn't any rain, we shouldn't really know what the sun was for". And Barley and Hetty nodded their bedraggled bonnets in absolute agreement.

There was no real sense of hurry because they knew that Lamfrey was still two nights away, and they had to stop first at Hawk's Corner, for Dyke to pace and set the post to rights. They reached it just after noon and it took the rest of the day for Hetty and Barley to set up the encampment and Dyke to work at the sign itself. It was one of his favourites, a hawk with spread wings and curved beak pointing the way to Egglestone. He had carved it in the cave three years back during a spell of thunderstorms, and even now you could almost feel the lightning in the tilt of its head and fierce curve of the beak.

The cave itself made Hawk's Corner one of Barley's own favourite stopping places. It was half-way up the rocky hillside that overlooked the road, its entrance hidden by huge, whitish boulders and later in the year by foxgloves growing in low purple forests. It was only a small cave, cosy and dry enough even for Hetty, who didn't really hold with caves. She always refused to sleep in the others that Barley found from time to time on their travels. After a brief sniff round them she would always pronounce them damp, draughty, and generally bad for the bones.

"Apart from which," she would say, "there's always a chance of the roof dropping in. And there's no danger of the sky doing *that*. Not yet, leastways."

She took a real pride in this particular one, though, and made it so much like home that the Signposters were always sorry to leave it. That night they sat in the mouth of the cave savouring their hot cheese cakes and the strangeness of their new dwelling. If Barley looked behind her she saw the firelight moving on the reddish-brown walls of rock. Looking outwards, she seemed on a level with the sky and stars that rolled about, above and even, it seemed, below her. Afterwards she tried to lie awake on her straw mattress watching the slow, dying dance of the fire on the rough ceiling. But the flames only tugged her unwillingly towards sleep, and all of a sudden it was morning and the mouth of the cave was filled with a red dawn.

Dyke's pacing was a long one, so he made an early start.

"Fifty-nine furlongs it says on the sign," he said glumly. "More like seventy, that means. Legs like ladders that man must've had."

Hetty clucked and pushed an extra oatie into his pocket, and Barley danced off at his side to see him on the first few miles of his journey. It was not that she thought he might be lonely. Dyke and his thoughts made good company on a long pace. Barley always felt that if she were on the move things were much more likely to happen than if she stayed still, even in a cave, waiting for them.

Walking with Dyke on a pace was not a very sociable affair, because of the counting that went on under his breath the whole time. At the end of a furlong he might come out with an odd remark, after first having chalked a mark on his slate, but then he would be off again straight away, striding and muttering towards the next signpost. Barley had a hard job to keep up with him because he really did stride out as far as his legs would allow him, in an attempt to keep his own reckonings as near Connery's as he could.

"Folks don't like it if places keep getting further and further away," he would say. "It's not natural, and you can't blame 'em."

This particular morning Barley was quite out of breath after the first eleven furlongs and was about to turn back when she spied a figure approaching them on foot.

"It's Quill!" she cried, recognizing the strange tumbling walk and bulging shoulder-pack.

"Two hundred and eighteen, nineteen, twenty. So it is," agreed Dyke, marking his slate.

They waited exactly where they were until he came up to them. It was not worth Dyke's while to begin another furlong and risk losing count.

"Good day," Quill greeted them, dropping his pack. "Roads cross. We meet again."

"Aye. And where are you bound?" Dyke asked. The pedlar told him.

"And you?"

"Lamfrey," said Dyke. "The Makers are Family, you know."

Quill nodded. He surveyed Barley with his dark bright eyes.

"I come from Lamfrey," he said. "There are surprises there."

"Surprises?" asked Barley and Dyke together.

The pedlar shouldered his pack again. He never seemed able to stop still, it was as if he must always be tumbling forward to the next place, in spite of himself. He stared at Barley again.

"The strolling players are in Lamfrey," he remarked abruptly. "Good day. Good fortune."

He was off so suddenly that Dyke and Barley could only call their farewells to his back.

"Turn back now, Barley," suggested Dyke. "You could walk along with him."

Barley shook her head.

"He goes too fast," she said. "I should never keep up."

Besides, Quill spoke little. He went tiptoe as if he were in flight, lonely as a bird.

She walked slowly back to the cave. Hetty was brushing it out with her broom made of twigs. Barley could see the cloud of reddish dust nearly half a mile away, and knew that before long she would be able to hear the singing too.

"There's been folks in this cave," said Hetty, red-faced and hot and thoroughly enjoying herself, "There's been a fire."

"I suppose other people must know about it as well as us," said Barley. But she had always thought of the cave as her own, because she had found it, and was not pleased to think that strangers had been there.

"There's this as well," said Hetty, holding out her hand.

It was a small leather bag, the kind that most boys carried to hold their marbles. But looking at this particular one made Barley suddenly sad. The yellowish leather and fringed thongs put her in mind of Kit, who had one just like it.

"You may as well keep it," said Hetty.

Barley was not at all sure that she wanted to. Being reminded of Kit was going to be sad this year. But she took it all the same and put it in the big wicker basket with the rest of her belongings. Then she seized the broom that Hetty had dropped and began to sweep furiously till Hetty coughed and sneezed and threw her apron over her face and at last ran out into the open away from the swirling dust.

But the trick worked. Ten minutes later Kit was forgotten and Barley was happy again. There was still tomorrow, and the Lamfrey Makers.

# Chapter Eight

Towards evening on the following day the Signposters drove into Lamfrey. Low golden sunlight was still flooding the streets, and they seemed more than usually alive, thronged with bustling and excited people.

In the market-place the Signposters saw the reason for it all. Two wide, flat carts had been drawn up side by side and even now were being made into a stage. The people of Lamfrey jostled round to watch the players hammering, erecting wooden trees and houses, and unloading costumes from their great hampers.

"The strolling players!" cried Barley. "Oh, can we watch them?"

"Tonight, perhaps," said Hetty unexpectedly. Usually Barley was not allowed to stay up so late, but the stir of Lamfrey was already working on Hetty. She sat up very straight, a spot of red on each cheek and her eyes darting like a bird's.

The Lamfrey Makers lived in a narrow street leading off the market-place called Fetter Lane. They occupied three tall houses joined together, with big windows on the street to display their wares. Almost before Cornish had stopped Barley was clambering from the wagon and peering in and then calling, "Oh! It's hobby horses! Come and look!"

The window was full of them, some carved out of wood and painted dapple or white, with wicked eyes and scarlet reins with bells. Others were cunningly made of stuffed rags or leather or straw, but each and every one of them was different, even to the poles.

Behind them, sitting on a low stool, needle and thread in hand, was Penelope, the Lamfrey grandmother. Barley opened the door, bells jangled, and the next minute Penelope had dropped her tapestry, and was standing, arms outstretched, to catch Barley. Then the bells were jangling again and Dyke and Hetty were both talking at once and Penelope threw up her hands and cried "Mercy!"

With that, she sat down and picked up her tapestry again, her old fingers twitching for the rhythm of the needle and her dim eyes hungry for the bright silks.

"You know where they are," she said, smiling.

The Signposters did. Behind the houses was a large wooden building that was the Makers' workroom. They hurried over the cobbled yard, pushed open the door, and next minute were surrounded by the Makers.

Barley stood close to Hetty's side and let the noise and excitement wash over her. It was like this every year. Looking round with dazed eyes she found that she still could not remember all their names, but that still it did not seem to matter, because a Maker was a Maker, and that was really all there was to it.

Now they were all wild-eyed and astonished, talking in high eager voices and alive and crackling to their fingertips. Soon, at work again, they would all be silent, each Maker in his own private pool of quiet, eyes intent or dreaming, only the fingers ceaselessly moving. It seemed then to Barley that they were all eyes and fingers.

At last the greetings were over and Dyke was by now as flushed and bright-eyed as Hetty herself. Nowhere else in Flockshire did he find so many Smiths under one roof. This, indeed, was Family. But because he was an artist himself, he began to move towards the door.

"We shall see you all at supper," he said. "I've news for you."

"News!" The Makers raised their eyebrows and whispered one to another, "What can it be? News! News!"

But by the time the Signposters had reached the door and were closing it softly behind them, the workroom was quiet again and the Makers' heads were bent.

In the big warm kitchen the Signposters found one of the Makers taking her turn at cooking supper. It was Ellen, and she was carefully putting the currant eyes into gingerbread men. Even when the Makers were cooking they ran to extravagance. Every meal was different. Barley remembered last year's pie-crust decorated with the names of all the Makers, and the cake to follow made in the shape of a castle, with marzipan flags flying from the turrets.

"It's the Signposters!" cried Ellen now with delight. She pushed the trays of gingerbread men into the oven and turned to greet them.

"And look at Barley! Hasn't she grown?"

Relatives who only see one once a year always exclaim about this, Barley had found. They never seemed able to believe that so much growing had taken place without them.

Ellen rinsed her floury hands and took the Signposters' things, and they all sat round the scrubbed table with as much Family Feeling as anyone could wish for. Dyke could not stop beaming. But the best moment for Barley came later, when the Makers had finished work and eaten their meal. When Dyke had told his idea, and all the Makers had promised to come, and after Pen's letter had been read aloud and exclaimed over, one of the Makers said:

"All turn to to tidy up, and we'll be off to the market."

"Market!" exclaimed Hetty. "At this time of night? It's nearly dark."

"Market-place," he explained. "The strolling players. We don't miss them. Never."

"Oh," said Hetty, taken aback. "You all go, do you?"

"All of us. Man, woman and child."

"That's me!" cried Barley joyfully. "Oh, let's go too. You said we might."

"O-o-oh," said Hetty. "Well, let's then. No harm."

After that the women were bustling about clearing the dishes and finding their best bonnets and shawls. All the Makers liked dressing up, and they ran to a good many feathers and brooches and sequins and trimmings of all sorts. Hetty, who was a plain, no-nonsense dresser herself, sometimes said she thought them rather showy. But secretly Barley admired them, and intended to dress exactly the same herself when she was grown up.

Tonight she accepted the offer of some blue glass beads and a string of crocheted daisies to "liven up your bonnet". She then slipped past Hetty's disapproving eyes and went with Dyke into the street.

The air was warm and soft and springlike, it flowed like water over Barley's cheeks. The fiery heads of torches bobbing along towards the market-place, and the hum and jostle of a town astir, filled her with a choking excitement. In the market it was nearly as light as day, but the light itself was all moving, leaping and licking up towards the stars that shrank into a pale smoke before it.

All Lamfrey was abroad tonight. It was like a fair day. Country folk sat by their stalls or crouched over charcoal fires, toasting cheese for a halfpenny or roasting potatoes or dipping apples in thick brown toffee, two for a penny. Barley and Dyke had one apiece and joined the crowd that was already collecting round the two wide wagons.

As they did so, a strange figure bounded suddenly out from behind the draperies, and a gasp went up from the crowd.

"Oh dear!" cried Barley, "it's starting! Mother will be late!"

"It's a warmer upper," explained Dyke, "not the play proper. Look—ah, look! Did you see that?"

The strange figure was turning cartwheels across the stage and as it straightened up Barley saw that it was a man or boy dressed as a cat. It was clad from top to toe in black fur. It wore a mask with pointed ears, whiskers and narrow green eyes. For a moment it stood there, poised on tiptoe in the leaping rushlight. Something silver glinted among the fur, and Barley stared, suddenly caught by it. In the same moment, she remembered Quill and his strange words.

Like a cat the figure leapt nimbly up to sway right out above the crowd, swinging along the wooden beams, dropping neatly on to an upturned crate and from there with a spring back on to the stage and out of sight. Then Barley felt her sleeve tugged as Hetty arrived breathlessly beside her, and at the same moment the play began.

But after the play was finished, the cat came back a second time, and Barley, seeing again the glint of silver among the fur, and remembering again Quill's words, and half-remembering a dozen other things, suddenly *knew*. As the cat, with a final flick of its tail, leapt out of sight, Barley let go of Dyke's hand and began to push her way frantically through the crowd.

"Here, Barley!" she heard him call. But she took no notice. With a gasp she reached the edge of the crowd and hurried to the back of the stage, where she caught a glimpse of the masked cat jumping into a covered wagon. She reached it just as the canvas flaps were drawn together. Quickly she looked round. No one was near. She stood as close to the wagon as she could and stretching up towards the faint crack of light between the flaps, she whispered loudly:

"Kit! Kit!"

There was no reply. Barley waited, then climbed the steps and peered in. No one was there. But in that very moment her sharp ears caught the faintest of muffled thuds, and running to the door she saw the dark figure of the cat leaping from the other end of the wagon.

"Kit!" she cried.

He was gone, bounding over the gleaming cobbles and swiftly lost in the shadow. She stared after him, and heard a burst of music and cheers as the players made their last farewells to Lamfrey. She knew that it was no use chasing him—they had run too many races together in the old days. Slowly she made her way back to the market-place. The curtains of the stage were drawn and the rushlights were being snuffed out one by one. As the redhaired torches wove their ways homewards, the stars were coming into their own again, magically bright and silver above the roof-tops.

She saw Dyke and Hetty waiting, and could hear the Makers calling and laughing as they hurried away.

"Where have you been, child?" cried Hetty, hurrying towards her. "You're as white as wax. What's amiss?"

"Nothing, mother. I'm cold, that's all. Let's go home."

"Aye, we'd best," said Dyke, his quick eyes seeing Barley's misery. "We'll be lost here in the dark if we don't make haste."

So the three of them followed the beckoning lights of the Makers, with no more questions asked. And when they came blinking into the light and warmth of the house on Fetter Lane, they found that there was to be a party. Once the Makers were excited and all dressed up, they could never go to bed without having a party.

There were games, goodies, charades and forfeits. Barley was not in the mood for any of them, but at least there were no questions. When she climbed the ladder to bed at last, she rummaged in her hamper for the bag Hetty had found in the cave. She went to bed with her fingers curled about it, because after all the doings of the day, without it she could hardly believe that she had found Kit, only to lose him again.

# Chapter Nine

Barley was perched in an elm-tree when she saw the army coming. It was two weeks now since they had left Lamfrey, and May was beginning. She sat in a shower of leaves while the wind rocked the springy branches and the twigs were pattering about her.

She was up an elm-tree partly because she liked being up trees and partly because she was on the look-out for Dyke, expected back from a pacing at any minute. Hetty was making camp up on the hillside by the stream, because there were no villages anywhere near. Barley was glad. She was glad for a few days to get back into the old, carefree rhythm of signposting. It seemed to her (though she was a little ashamed of the thought, and would never have voiced it) that this season there had been altogether too many Flockshire Smiths for real comfort. Usually they managed to strike a very happy balance between Family and Signposting, but this year Dyke was threading his way through Flockshire from Smith to Smith with hardly a thought for his posts. So far he had done only one carving, and that merely a very simple cock, just a cut-out really, no feather or elaborate curling of comb as you would have expected.

Even Hetty had noticed.

"Don't you go grudging your posts, now," she had warned. "You'll be sorry, after."

She had been in a bad mood that day, just back from a visit to her old aunt at Firbeck, who still called her Lettice and had asked if she was married yet. Barley could see

that she was discouraged and not really in a Family mood at all.

Even now Dyke was returning from a pace that had taken him to Smiths. It was one of the largest families of all, and the head of it, one of Dyke's cousins, was a sheepfarmer in a very out of the way spot. There were eleven children, and Hetty always said that it wasn't so much a family he was after, as a flock.

Barley was leaning her back against the trunk of the tree and gazing up through the half-furled leaves to the changing flecks of blue sky beyond. In the end it made her a little dizzy, seasick almost. She lifted her head to scan the road again, and saw the army. Her eyes widened at the sight of flags and banners, men on horseback and the flashing silver of armour. The tramp, tramp of marching men reached her ears.

She herself was not at war with anyone, but the faintest of shivers ran down her spine.

Barley was not a coward, and there was nothing really to be afraid of in the sight of an approaching army. It was the steady tramp, tramp of the feet that threw her into a panic. She knew that they were not coming for her. It simply *sounded* as if they were.

If she left the tree, she would have to cross their path to reach Hetty and the safety of the encampment. She huddled back against the strong spine of the tree and wished that the half-open leaves would by some miracle unfurl and screen her utterly. Her heart was thudding now in rhythm with the approaching feet. The first riders were close enough for her to see their stern faces under the helmets and the embroidered crests on their tunics. She sat clenched, waiting.

The leaders were passing her now, but at that very moment, when danger was at its height, a voice cried, "Halt!" and the whole procession came to a standstill before Barley's horrified eyes. There was a short discussion and then two men wheeled back down the file, giving orders, and Barley, straining her ears, caught the word "camp".

They were going to make camp at that very spot. The same stream as the one the Signposters had settled by higher up the hill, ran through the clearing. Men were already unharnessing the horses and leading them to it. Soon she was surrounded by swarming soldiers, calling in loud voices, throwing off their armour, beginning to light fires.

Barley sat staring, unable to move. She did not see how she could ever get away. I shall have to stay here till they go, she thought. It might be days. Days and days.

The rough bark was beginning to cut her legs and it was growing cold as the sun dropped and the wind still blew. But she did not dare climb down. Their roughness and noise terrified her and made her dizzy.

And then, out of all the babble of voices, a familiar one came floating up, impossible yet unmistakable. She craned forward, disbelieving. It was Dyke, wandering into the encampment, nodding to left and right, for all the world as if he were a baron inspecting his private army.

"Father!"

Barley let out a shriek and dropped so hastily from her perch that she tore her skirt from hem to waist and a nearby soldier spilled half his soup. The next minute she was clutching Dyke's cloak and sobbing and laughing at the same time, and Dyke was saying, "Here, here, what's all this?" and the captain said, "Where's *that* little maid dropped out of?"

After that, with Dyke safe and familiar beside her, Barley could soon peep out from among the folds of his cloak and find that the soldiers had friendly faces, after all, and that the armour they wore was only a disguise.

She was still glad when Dyke made his farewells and they set off up the hillside towards their own camp. When she glimpsed Hetty's tall figure, pinafore flapping, stooping over the cauldron, she raced on ahead to give her a hug that took her by surprise and made her say:

"Now, then! Is it my birthday?"

By the time they were seated comfortably round on their straw mats, the dark was prowling around them and Barley gave a sigh of thanks for the warm, golden ring of their own fire, and the plate of savoury broth that Hetty set before her. Below them they could see the fires of the soldiers, and every now and then voices and music were blown up to them on sudden gusts.

"What's that army doing down there?" Hetty enquired suspiciously, when Dyke had drunk enough broth to put him in the mood for conversation. "I don't like armies about, and never did."

"Oh, they're not at war," Dyke told her. "They're just back from over the sea. Been fighting foreigners. I forget which, but foreigners, anyhow."

Hetty sniffed and pretended to look uninterested, but before long her curiosity got the better of her, and she asked, "Did they win?"

"Oh, yes," said Dyke. "But they're very tired. They're making camp down there for a few days to rest the men and horses."

"Thank goodness we're off tomorrow then," said Hetty. "If there's one thing I detest, it's to be woke up with an army on my doorstep. And it's woke up we will be, make no mistake. All that bugling. I don't *like* armies."

Barley secretly agreed with her. She still remembered her anguish in the elm, the tramping feet, the rough voices and heavy clang of armour.

"How did the pace go, then?" enquired Hetty, changing the subject with the plates and dishing up a hot, fruity pudding that had been boiling since noon, keeping Barley's nose on the twitch with its spicy steam.

"Fair," Dyke's voice was glum. Hetty looked sharply at him.

"Much out?" she asked. "That dratted Connery."

"No, not more than you'd expect," said Dyke, digging at his pudding in a depressed way that annoyed Hetty, who liked to see her meals done justice to.

"Well, then," she retorted, "what's all this drooping for?"

Dyke was silent.

"It's Family!" she said suddenly. "That's what it is. Else you'd tell me straight out. Isn't it?"

"Well, then, Hetty, it is," admitted Dyke.

"It's that sheep-shearing shepherd of yours," continued Hetty triumphantly. "He won't come to Ingle at Michaelmas. Now then, I've hit on it, haven't I?"

"Half," agreed Dyke miserably. "Half hit on it."

"Well, then," challenged Hetty, "what about the other half?"

"Not won't, *can't*!" burst out Dyke then. "He says he *can't*."

"Well!" exclaimed Hetty. "I've never heard the like. As if a few silly sheep can't nibble their grass for a few days without *him* standing over them. Sheep isn't my favourite creatures, and never will be, but one thing I hope *can* be said for them, and that is that they can nibble a bit of grass without—"

"Hetty!" Dyke had already tried to interrupt her once and failed. "Hetty, it ain't that. It ain't that at all."

"What is it, then, father?" asked Barley, who hated to see Dyke so thoroughly downcast.

"It's the family," said Dyke. "Fourteen of them there is now."

"Oh lawks!" cried Hetty, "Another!"

"And they don't see how they're to stop at Ingle, for there's no room, d'ye see. And they're right, Het. You know how Ingle is at fair time. Houses full up to the chimneys, and folks bedding in the stables. And *fourteen*, Hetty."

Hetty stared at him, for once nonplussed.

"And that's not all," went on Dyke. "I've been thinking on it on the way back. One hundred and twenty-seven—I mean eight—Family. They've all to find lodging. Oh Hetty, they never will. Never!"

Barley, watching his face pinched with disappointment in the firelight, wondered for a moment if he had let go of his dream. But as she looked, he lifted his head and looked straight at them and said:

"But there's an answer. If you pry and ferret and turn things over, there's an answer to everything. It's just a bit of a hurdle, that's all, that needs jumping over."

Barley thought that a roof to cover a hundred and twenty-eight Flockshire Smiths was more than just a hurdle. But seeing Dyke's eyes suddenly reflect the fire's blaze, she knew that the dream was safe, and believed him. There was an answer. But she did not know that she was to be the one to find it.

# Chapter Ten

Next morning, as Hetty had predicted, the buglers blew early as any cock and twice as loud.

"Drat them," said Hetty, banging her pots as she made breakfast. She was an early riser by nature, and the fact that the last pale stars had hardly faded from the sky did not bother her at all. It was "all that blowing and screeching" as she put it.

"Frightening the birds, poor things, till their whistles stick in their throats, and no wonder."

It was a grey, cloudy morning, and none of the Signposters was in very high spirits. Dyke was evidently still brooding over Family affairs, and Barley caught his mood and began to wonder whether the whole thing was not hopeless after all, and best given up.

They sat hunched round a poor fire, chewing steadily, wordless and melancholy as if by unspoken agreement. Hetty was wearing her black apron, which was always a bad sign. She wore it whenever she wished to work off her feelings by doing all sorts of dirty and disagreeable jobs.

"She'll probably want to wash the whole wagon down," thought Barley glumly. "And then we shan't get started before dinner."

"I shall wash the wagon down this morning," announced Hetty, interrupting Barley's thoughts. "It's a downright disgrace. We may *live* like vagrants, but we're respectable folk, and can drive a wagon that looks as if we was, I hope."

Dyke did not attempt to dissuade her.

"In that case, Hetty," he said, "I may as well pace to Foxes Bridge."

Barley would have offered to go with him, but she knew that he wanted to be alone with his thoughts, to dwell on the problem of a roof for the Flockshire Smiths. He would brood and brood over the problem, probably for days on end, and then the answer would come all of a sudden, quite unexpectedly while he was tying his boot-laces or just drawing in his breath to whistle. It was always like that with Dyke. And always the answers he got were exactly right, perfect.

Hetty would often marvel at his inspirations.

"You've got a real gift for it, Dyke," she would say, "the ideas you get—clear out of the blue."

"Ah, but it's the thinking beforehand that counts," Dyke would try to explain. "It *looks* as if the idea comes out of the blue, but it don't. It comes of the thinking I've done beforehand."

Hetty refused to allow his miraculous powers to be explained away in so simple a fashion.

"*I* think," she would say, "but I don't get ideas."

And this statement always concluded the argument.

Dyke's pace was only a short one, so he carved himself a thick slice of bread and cheese and said:

"Back for dinner, Het," and prepared to be off.

"You'll need your cape," said Hetty. "It's going to rain."

"Not this morning," said Dyke. "I'll be back before the rain comes."

That was where he was wrong. By ten o'clock the sky was a low-hanging grey and the wind smelt wet and fresh. Hetty lifted her head and sniffed at it like a fox or badger, then resumed her scrubbing with renewed frenzy.

Barley, to her relief, had not been allowed to help. She had prepared the stew and made some oaties, in all kinds of shapes and sizes, as she thought the Makers might have done. Hetty had swept her eyes over the collection of hens, rabbits, stars and daisies (all a rather greyish white, from much kneading) with a sharp shake of the head.

"Fancy is as fancy *tastes*," she had remarked. "As regards cooking, at any rate."

She really did seem impossible to please that day. Barley would have wandered off for a walk, but the army was still swarming below them at the foot of the hill. It was a pity, because Barley liked above all things to follow a stream, and this one went splashing down between the wind-bent grasses as if it were beckoning her in its wake. She gazed down to where the horses were tethered by its banks, and next moment gave a little cry:

"Mother! Look!"

Hetty turned and looked over her shoulder, still scrubbing. Then she dropped her brush and advanced to Barley's side, wiping her hands on her apron. Both stood looking on to the sudden blossoming of colour into that grey morning.

"Tents," said Hetty at last, unnecessarily.

Four of them there were, struggling to unfurl, and even as Hetty and Barley watched one of them all at once rose and billowed and spread its crimson skirt.

"Oh, the size of it!" exclaimed Hetty. "Fancy a tent the size of that!"

They stood watching until all four giant tents were in full bloom, straining and tugging at their ropes as if now they were ready to take to the air.

Hetty shivered suddenly and hugged her arms as if she were drawing a shawl round her shoulders. Then she looked up at the sky.

"Them tents," she said, "hasn't been put up a minute too soon. Rain to put the fire out, there'll be."

Ten minutes later the rain came. Barley ran swiftly round the fire snatching up her oaties from the hot stones where already the drops were hissing into steam. Hetty threw her cloak over her head and ran to where the blankets were wildly flapping from her clothes-line.

She hurled them ahead of her into the wagon and scrambled up herself, her skirts about her ears. She wiped her face on her pinafore and then she and Barley sat side by side looking out through a rain so heavy that the soldiers' tents were only a blur of colour far below, and the road taken by Dyke was curtained almost from view.

"I said he should have taken his cape," said Hetty gloomily. "*What* his bones'll suffer after this."

A few minutes later she observed, "Fire's near out. And you've left the lid off again, Barley. There'll be rain-water in the stew."

Then she relapsed into silence. But the constant drumming of the rain on the canvas, and the feeling of cosiness in being snug under their own roof out of the wind and wet, made the silence a companionable one. Slowly the drumming turned to a patter, the haze thinned and the crimson and blue and yellow of the tents swam into focus again.

"We'd best be off after dinner," said Hetty. "That army'll be here for weeks, or they wouldn't go putting up tents as big as town halls. We don't want mixing up in any wars."

She turned away and began to rummage round inside the wagon, finding the box that served as a table and laying out the bowls and spoons. Barley stayed staring down at the encampment, a little puzzled frown furrowing her brow.

All of a sudden, those giant tents seemed familiar. She had the strangest feeling that she had seen them before. Not that she could have done, of course. She had never in her life seen tents like these. Looking down on them from her perch in the wagon, she thought they looked like brilliantly coloured mushrooms.

Again she had that strange sensation of being on the verge of remembering something. Mushrooms. Or umbrellas. That was it. They reminded her of the giant umbrella she had always imagined when she wanted to see the Flockshire Smiths all together, as a Family.

And in the instant of remembering, she had the idea, a real, bolt-out-of-the-blue idea, worthy of Dyke himself. Catching sight of Dyke approaching up the hillside, his face bent against the rain, Barley jumped down and ran to meet him, pell mell, lifting her skirts and feeling the wet soaking into her stockings. She heard Hetty's voice calling after her, "Barley! You come back this instant!"

But Barley possessed by an idea was her father's daughter, and she kept on, right into Dyke's arms out-stretched to meet her.

# Chapter Eleven

At dinner the Signposters were so taken up by Barley's idea that the rainwater in the gravy was not even noticed, let alone remarked upon.

At first all was admiration and excitement.

"Fancy you coming to think of that!" exclaimed Hetty. "And yet, now you *do* think of it, the wonder of it is that it didn't strike us all. Plain as the nose on your face."

"We can have the ten-acre field behind Pen," planned Dyke. "Every manjack of the Flockshire Smiths can be under the very same roof. Think of that! Not just in Ingle, but under the very same roof!"

"They can," agreed Hetty, "but I think there should be two tents, Dyke. One for the men, and one for the women and children. As they might not all *want* to tent, Dyke. They'll have their own wagons, remember."

Dyke's face dropped a little, and Barley too felt disappointed, because her own private dream of the giant umbrella had seemed so very nearly about to come true. There was something so right, so *perfect*, about the idea of all the Flockshire Smiths under one giant canvas.

"We could have a party," said Hetty, "*That* could be in one tent."

"Yes!" cried Dyke and Barley together. "That's it!"

"To Family!" cried Dyke, brandishing his mug of wine and becoming lightheaded at the very prospect of it all.

Once the arrangements had been agreed upon and the Signposters were feeling agreeably victorious and more than a little clever, Hetty began to see all kinds of difficulties and drawbacks. It was not that she wanted to be a wet blanket. It was just that she had a very sensible, practical nature, and saw snags that were quite invisible to the dreamers of the family like Dyke and Barley.

"There's one thing," she started off. "Drat that fire. There's no hot water and grease on all the pots. There's one thing."

"What?" enquired Dyke absently, taking the sack of oats that hung from the side of the wagon.

"Tents is certainly perfect," said Hetty. "Just the thing. And we've a tent or two ourselves, and so've most folks."

"Why, that's right, Hetty," agreed Dyke amiably. "I'll just peg over and give Cornish his oats."

"*But*," said Hetty, holding up her hand to signal him to stop, "our tents ain't as big as town halls. And nor is most folks'."

Dyke stared at her.

"The only tents *I* ever see as big as town halls," said Hetty, "is *those*."

She pointed her finger down towards the army's encampment. Then, having said her piece, squatted down and began rubbing at the pots with wet grass in an effort to remove some of the grease. Once Hetty had *found* problems, her part of the work was done. It was for Dyke to solve them.

"I'll go down there right away," said Dyke then, with

an effort at firmness but an uncertainty in his voice that even Barley noticed.

"You don't think they'll go *giving* them to you, do you?" said Hetty. "I hope."

"They might," said Dyke defiantly. "Or trade them."

"Oh dear, Dyke," said Hetty straightening up, "you *are* a child. You'd think you could have the moon if you took a fancy to it."

Dyke did not reply.

"Just wait while I get my bonnet," she went on. "And *I'll* go down. This is going to need some common sense, Dyke."

"Yes, Hetty," said Dyke humbly.

"But you don't like armies, mother," cried Barley, alarmed at the thought of Hetty descending alone into that vast encampment.

"What I like," said Hetty, "and what I *do*, is often two entirely opposite things."

With this she climbed back into the wagon and stayed in there for about twenty minutes while Barley and Dyke fed Cornish and rubbed down his rough coat.

When she came out she was a magnificent figure. She wore her best fur trimmed cloak over her dark green velvet, and her bonnet was enormous and of such importance that she kept it in a special box hanging from the roof of the wagon, like a cheese or ham. She carried a new bottle-green umbrella the Makers had given her with a fox's head carved on the handle.

"I'm off," she announced, and immediately was.

It was not only the clothes that gave Hetty such an air. It was the lift of her chin and the forward thrust of her laced boots as she began the descent. The hill was so steep that she had to do a kind of dignified goose-step in order to keep upright. Barley watched her admiringly. She knew that Hetty did not really want to go, and was only doing it for Dyke's sake. Dyke himself cleared his throat and said, "She's a good Signposter, your mother"—the highest praise of which he was capable.

After an hour Hetty still had not returned. By then both Dyke and Barley had finished all the little jobs they had invented to pass the time, and were feeling restless and even a little worried.

"Hetty does let her tongue go a bit," remarked Dyke. "But she's been gone a fairish while even considering that. I'll go down and look after her."

"We'll both go," said Barley. "I'll fetch my bonnet."

She was inside the wagon when Dyke called, "Barley, she's coming!"

So she was, and not alone. A strange little procession was mounting the hillside. Hetty came first, one hand clutching her bonnet, the other stabbing her umbrella into the turf ahead of her like a climbing stick. Behind her came three men, one behind the other, shouldering a long parcel like a rolled-up carpet.

"It's a tent!" gasped Dyke. "Blessed if she ain't brought a tent back with her!"

"She can't have!" cried Barley.

"What a marvel that woman is! Look at them there, tame as mice, heaving that parcel after her."

Barley swelled with pride. The everyday Hetty with flapping pinafore, sleeves rolled to the elbow and hair flying in long wisps, was transformed into a heroine, a worker of miracles. And seeing her mother in this new light, when Hetty finally puffed to a standstill, face flushed and bonnet determinedly awry, Barley felt almost shy of her.

"Where shall we put it, Ma'am?" asked the first soldier respectfully.

Hetty gestured with the fox's head.

"In the wagon," she said. "With a little care, if you please."

She watched while the rolled-up pillar of tent was stowed into the wagon, then inclined her head.

"Well done," she said. "You may tell Henry—Captain Brand—that I said so."

"Yes, Ma'am." The three men touched their caps. Barley gaped.

"Good day, Ma'am. Good day, Master and Miss."

"Good day. And thank you." Hetty stood even more than usually upright and nodded her large bonnet in reply to their salute.

"Well!" said Dyke when they were out of earshot. "That was a day's work, Hetty."

"It was, Dyke," Hetty nodded, her eyes still following the retreating soldiers.

"Did they *give* you the tent, mother?" asked Barley. It seemed hardly possible.

"What? Oh, yes," said Hetty carelessly. She seemed very little concerned about the tent. In fact she was most mysteriously contented. She wore a little pleased smile and a far-away look that seemed to have nothing at all to do with the tent. It was very unlike Hetty to look moonstruck. Barley and Dyke exchanged enquiring glances.

"It's a wonder they didn't give you a pair," said Dyke jocularly.

"Oh, the other one's all arranged," said Hetty dreamily. Her eyes were still fixed on the encampment below. "There's a message going to Lamfrey by one of the riders. The Makers'll do another for us, Dyke."

"Of course!" cried Dyke joyfully. "The Makers! You *are* full of ideas, Hetty."

"Oh, it wasn't my idea," said Hetty. "*I* don't get ideas. It was Captain Brand's—Henry's."

"Henry?" said Dyke. "Did you know him, then, Hetty?"

Hetty turned then, and her eyes were full of amazed delight.

"Oh Dyke!" she cried. "Oh Barley! It's *Cousin* Henry! The lost Henry! Oh Dyke, I've found some family of my own!"

While Dyke and Barley stared with mouths ajar, she pulled the enormous bonnet off, sat abruptly on the wet grass, and burst into tears.

# Chapter Twelve

Finding a relative of her own, a real one, who never mistook her for a Lettice or even forgot entirely who she was, made a new woman of Hetty. Barley and Dyke watched the transformation with delighted wonder. It was not that Hetty had ever been sour or brooding. But now she was positively alight with uncontained pleasure As for the Michaelmas Reunion, she was more bent on it than ever. Gone were her gloomy misgivings and dark hints of failure.

"It's because she *knows* about Family now, d'ye see," Dyke explained one day to Barley as they watched Hetty trimming her bonnet with wild flowers and carolling loudly as she did so. "You've got to *be* Family to know the meaning of it."

"But *we're* her family," said Barley, rather hurt by the suggestion that up till now Hetty had been a forlorn, abandoned creature with no real kin of her own. "We're Family, and always have been."

She still privately thought that the deaf aunt at Firbeck and her prodigal son made a very thin family when compared with the teeming ramifications of the Smiths.

"Of *course* we're Family," nodded Dyke. "As snug a little family as you'll find anywhere. But it's the—oh—"

he spread his arms as if that were the only way he could express what he was trying to say. "It's the—"

He tailed off and his arms dropped to his sides. It was no use. Dyke's Family Feeling was something that could never be put into words. Oddly enough, his very failure to capture it made Barley exactly aware of what he meant. Dyke was never good at putting what he felt into words. Whenever he talked about the reunion to people all he ever said was, "It'll round off the season nicely, that's what we thought." Which, as a hint of Dyke's real feelings, was hardly a hint at all.

Hetty's new-found Family went straight off to see his mother at Firbeck as soon as the Signposters left their encampment.

"I should think she'll be surprised to see me," he observed, "after all these years."

"Twenty," said Dyke, his voice disapproving, despite himself. People who went off and left their Families for twenty years were little short of criminals to him, even if they did wear gold braid and command armies.

"Now you stop there," Hetty told her bewhiskered cousin. "No gadding off to wars again till I get back."

She hoped fervently that the deaf aunt would not call her son Cedric or Oswald and so dampen his spirits that he left home for another twenty years. She made him promise to stay. She intended to keep as firm a check on her Family as Dyke kept on his. Sometimes, in the evenings, as she sat by the fire sewing, she would drop her work and sit gazing into the flames. Then, "Think," she would sigh, "if he gets married!"

The possibilities were endless. Nephews, nieces, great-nephews, great-nieces . . .

"He might," Dyke would agree soberly. He too sat

counting children in the fire, peopling the future in his head.

So the summer passed. There were showery days that passed into weeks of still, cloudless heat, crackling storms and days spent hurrying from shelter to shelter. But whatever the weather, still Barley saw the year as a rising hill with Michaelmas Day crowning the summit, and the nearer they came to the top, the more her excitement mounted.

Mingled with the visits to Family, the happy planning and delicious expectation, were Barley's secret thoughts of Kit. Neither she nor Dyke and Hetty ever mentioned him. Nor did they speak of Uncle Wick and Aunt Mathilda, though Barley knew that they were the one splinter in the stew. As long as Wick remained stubborn then the reunion at Ingle would not be a real one at all. It would be a failure. Only on one occasion did Dyke bring the subject up.

"Perhaps he'll soften," was all he said. "Perhaps he'll send word to say he's coming."

But he spoke wistfully, as if he knew the impossibility of such a thing. Barley and Hetty were silent because they both knew it too.

September came, the wheat was gold, the blackberries reddened and birds flew in flocks now that the sun was thinning. Michaelmas Day was on the twenty-ninth. The Signposters were nearing the brow of the hill. From the farthest reaches of Flockshire they turned and began to retrace their steps towards Ingle.

Barley was always excited by autumn. The cold wet smell of dew and mists and the richer scents of fruits and seeding grasses went to her head every year as if they were everlastingly new and known for the first time.

Mixed with the exhilaration was the sadness of approaching winter. Autumn days on the road would be the last till spring.

One morning in mid-September Barley went running off after breakfast into a soft white mist that had crept up on them in the night. She could never resist going into the blurred secret and silent world of a mist. Once she was warm, and could feel the damp air finely brushing her hot cheeks, she stopped and listened. Everything was quite still, only the moisture dripped from leaf and bough. Birds never sing until a mist rises.

Then, quite suddenly, the mist *did* rise. It melted into a wide flood of pale light as the sun broke through. Barley had never seen a mist dissolve so quickly, it drew back and showed trees and bushes draped with the rags of cobwebs and lit by tiny candle-flames of dew.

And out of the ebbing tide of mist, pack on his back and head bent, came Quill the pedlar, as silently as his own shadow. It seemed to Barley that he would have passed right by without ever knowing she was there, had he not seen her long shadow on the road, lying in his path. He stopped and stared at it as it lay across his feet, then lifted his head at last to Barley herself.

"Roads cross," he said. "Good day."

"Good day, Quill," said Barley. She stood awkwardly, unable to think of another word to give the pedlar. He was not like other people. Quill spoke only with words of meaning, and Barley, knowing this, wisely said nothing at all.

"Tell Dyke to go to Bilbury," he said suddenly, regarding her with his brown eyes, quick as a bird's. "Our paths cross, and so I tell you."

He nodded and went, tumbling towards the sun and

the mist's end. Barley, looking after him, had the strangest
feeling that he had woven his path deliberately through
the mist to cross her shadow, and that though he was a
pedlar, his whole life was a pattern of paths crossing
wherever he meant them to.

Barley turned and began to run again, back towards
the encampment. Dyke was hanging out the blankets to
dry and Hetty was already blackberrying, her mouth
darkly red and hair pulled to wisps by the briars. Barley
stood there and both Dyke and Hetty turned to look at
her.

"You're back soon," observed Hetty. "Get a bowl,
Barley, do, and give a hand. I do detest to see them birds
feasting off what's perfectly good food for mortals. Three
pies we shall have from here if we pick before them birds,
and not so much as a thimbleful if we pick after."

"I met Quill," said Barley.

They looked at her, and once again she was aware of
the dew dropping around her, like the world's time tick-
ing away towards Michaelmas and the Day.

"He said, 'Tell Dyke to go to Bilbury.'"

Dyke and Hetty exchanged glances. For a moment
neither of them spoke. Then Dyke let out a loud whoop,
and began gathering the blankets together in armfuls,
bundling them again into the wagon.

"Bilbury!" he cried exultingly. "We're to go to Bilbury!"

Astonished, Barley went after him.

"But, father," she said, "are we going?"

"We're going!" cried Dyke. "Didn't I tell you, Hetty?
*Won't* I slap Wick's back! *Won't* I show him!"

To Barley it was suddenly clear that Dyke had been
wanting all along to go back to Bilbury. He wanted to

go back and clap Uncle Wick on the back and wring his pudgy hand and take all the blame for himself. He wanted to pour all the love and goodwill of his Family Feeling on to Uncle Wick, and the night of the storm was no more to him than a feather in the wind.

Barley and Hetty exchanged looks and shook their heads. Then Hetty began sensibly to put her things together.

"We'll stop by at Firbeck," she said. She could never feel quite easy in her mind that Cousin Henry had not tired of shouting into his mother's ear-trumpet and gone back to soldiering, despite his promise.

"And the Makers," put in Barley, "to see if the tent is finished."

"That tent," said Dyke, "finished or not, will be a *tent*."

Of that they all felt certain. They were so excited and busy that it was not until they were on the wagon, and travelling, that the Signposters began to wonder, each secretly, *why* Quill had crossed their path, and why they must go to visit Bilbury again, and Wick. And Barley, who alone had seen Quill come out of the mist to step across her very shadow, wondered most of all.

# Chapter Thirteen

"It'll be near dark again by the time we get there," observed Dyke.

"Pooh!" said Hetty, and went on ladling the stew.

The Signposters had stopped just outside Bilbury for their supper.

"We can't count on a bite there," Hetty had said firmly, "and we shall all feel better on full stomachs!"

Barley, whose own stomach had been turning uneasily most of the day, agreed. She dreaded the prospect of meeting Uncle Wick again, not so much for her own sake, as for Dyke's, who pinned so much faith on it. For his part, he had been whistling all day. He had been whistling, in fact, throughout the journey from Lamfrey, where they had stopped for a day to see the Makers and inspect the tent. But the Signposters had not been allowed to see it. The Makers had flocked together and blocked the way into their workroom, crying, "No, no! You're not to see! It's a secret!"

To Barley this was even more satisfying than a glimpse of the tent itself would have been. Only a tent beyond all tents could raise such excitement and secrecy in the Makers, to whom excitement and secrecy were their life's blood.

The low autumn light slanted through the trees in shafts and gave Dyke an oddly fitting halo as he said suddenly and astonishingly:

"And now then, Barley, what about Kit?"

She stared at him. It was impossible to speak.

"What are you going to tell Wick?"

Dyke carried on with his stew as if he were only mentioning the weather. "For Hetty and I don't know. But something you *must* tell him, Barley. You can't hide a son from his own father."

So they had known all the time. Not a word had been said, not a question asked, and yet they had known.

"Come on, now, Barley," said Hetty, "eat your stew. Don't badger the child, Dyke. Let her eat her supper."

"You know!" cried Barley. "How did you know?"

"*We* aren't blind," said Hetty. "We've got eyes in our heads. Who else could it be but Kit, dancing and prancing up there, the way he always did."

"*With* a silver medallion swinging round his neck," put in Dyke, "that your mother and I happened to give him for his christening."

"And with you coming back white as wax," went on Hetty, "and eyes red as fire next day with weeping. *We're* not blind."

Barley prodded her stew. Now that it was all out in the open she felt suddenly flat. Her great secret, that she had guarded so closely through the whole summer, turned out not to be a secret at all. At the same time she had a feeling of relief. Hetty and Dyke shared the burden with her now. After all, it was a burden, to keep a secret about a son from his own father, even if the father *was* Uncle Wick, for whom Barley cared less than two pins.

Dyke cleared his throat.

"We shall have to tell Wick," he said. "It's only right."

"We don't even know for sure it *was* Kit," said Barley stubbornly. To her, right or wrong, it seemed like a betrayal.

"Yes, we do," said Hetty decisively. "And Dyke's right. We shall have to tell."

"And Wick's not the man to have his son gypsying along with strolling players," said Dyke. "Kit'll be back here pouring candles before the year's out."

"Before the *month's* out," said Hetty.

Barley, who had known this all along, felt more dejected than ever now it had been put into words.

"I shan't tell him!" she cried.

"*I* shall," said Dyke.

"Your Aunt Mathilda will be pulling hairpins out again, that I *can* see," commented Hetty. She began to clear away the supper things. "Ah, well, at least we've got full stomachs this time, and it don't look like rain."

The allusion to the last visit did nothing to raise the Signposters' spirits. All the whistle went out of Dyke, and the last lap into Bilbury was as gloomy and foreboding as it had been that other time, on the wet spring night six months before when Wick had driven them out into the storm.

But Dyke's Family Feeling was not easily dampened, and never for very long. As the roofs of Bilbury appeared in the distance he flicked the reins and the rocking movement of Cornish's canter miraculously restored his whistle and spirits together.

At his side Barley sat practising taking in the deep breath she would need to blurt out what she knew of Kit, when the time came. She knew that she would have to do it. She dreaded the moment when they would alight from

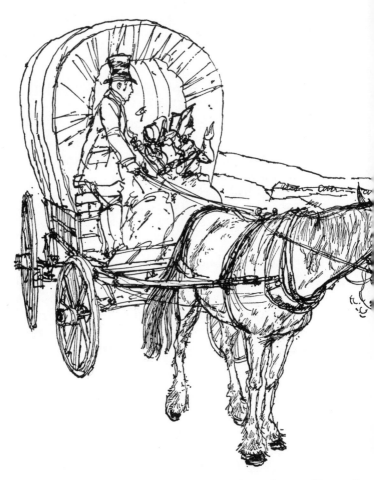

the wagon and knock on the door, when the rattling of bolts would begin and finally they would be face to face with Uncle Wick himself.

As it turned out, there was no door upon which to knock. Nor was there a house. There was bare earth, burned brownish black, there were charred stubs of

beams and piles of ashes, and here and there solid, un-reflecting puddles of wax.

The Signposters sat stunned and staring.

"Wick!" gasped Dyke at last, his eyes wide with horror and grief. "Oh Wick! What's become of him!"

"Oh Dyke, Dyke," moaned Hetty, rocking herself

from side to side and suddenly white. Barley clung to her mother's sleeve, frightened by the silence and emptiness where a house should have been.

"A house missing is a terrible shock," as Hetty used to say later. "You just don't *expect* to come round a corner and find a house gone."

"Wick!" shouted Dyke suddenly and loudly.

Hetty and Barley stared at him, thinking he must have gone clear out of his wits. The ashes of Wick's house had been cold for many a day, and the wind had blown them into grey drifts. Dyke's voice rang thin and hollow in the dusk.

"Wick!"

Then, impossibly, there came an answer.

"Dyke! Why, it's Dyke! Mathilda, it's Dyke come!"

The Signposters wheeled in the direction of the voice and saw Uncle Wick stumbling out from between the flaps of a tent pitched in what once had been his vegetable garden. Behind him came Aunt Mathilda, clutching at her hair and sobbing wildly. Surprised as she was, Barley had time to notice that Uncle Wick had gone thinner and his eyes were not so small, and that Aunt Mathilda had snatched up her yellow rosebud shawl and was pulling it up over her shoulders in honour of her visitors.

Next minute, everything was just as Dyke had dreamed it, except that instead of him slapping Wick's back, Wick at the same time was slapping Dyke's, and wringing his hand and wheezing:

"Dyke! Dyke old fellow, it's good to see you. It's good, *good*!" over and over again.

Aunt Mathilda laid her head on Hetty's shoulder and sobbed, while Hetty's own tears ran unchecked down her cheeks. Barley, overwhelmed, wept with them.

It was, as Hetty said later, "The most feelingest thing in the whole world."

Then at last Dyke and Wick left off patting each other's backs and Aunt Mathilda's sobs began to settle into sniffs, and they all stood back and began to take stock of things.

"You'd best come in, Dyke and Hetty," said Wick, waving his hand towards the tent. "There's not much to offer, but what there is is yours."

Dyke beamed at him.

"Don't you go worrying about *that*, Wick," he said. "We shall soon see about that, my dear fellow. And as for tents, why, we spend half our lives in them—and not as second best to houses, either. Because we like 'em!"

"Dyke," said Wick then, in a puzzled voice, "do you know, the odd thing is, but just lately I've begun to feel *myself* liking it. I don't want to, but I don't seem able to help myself. I *like* it!"

"And me!" wailed Aunt Mathilda, threatening to go off into hysterics again, "*I* like it as well. At least, I think I do! Oh dear!"

"Now then," said Dyke, giving them both a gentle push towards the tent. "Let's all go and sit down and talk the thing over. Stop rubbing at your eyes, Mathilda, you'll spoil your pretty shawl."

The astonished Barley watched Aunt Mathilda obediently stop crying and follow Dyke meekly as a lamb into the tent. She and Hetty raised their eyebrows at each other clear up into their hair, and followed.

# Chapter Fourteen

Uncle Wick's house had burned down over a month before in a high wind after a spell of August heat.

"Dry as tinder everything was," said Wick. "And the place full of candles that I'd made against the winter. Autumn's always my big time for candles."

"We think the wind blew the curtain against a candle-flame," said Aunt Mathilda. "But we can't know for sure. We shall go to our graves not knowing."

They sat there, the pair of them on their upturned boxes, looking at last to Barley like real humans, with their wide worried eyes, crumpled clothes and vanished dignity.

"We just snatched up what we could and ran out," went on Wick. "But there was no saving anything much."

Aunt Mathilda pulled her yellow rosebud shawl more closely round her shoulders, and Barley pictured her running up the ladder to save it, snatching it up while the flames forked and the smoke flew round her in gusty billows.

"We stood outside and watched it burn," said Uncle Wick. "There was nothing else to do."

There was silence. None of the Signposters knew how to comfort a grief like this.

"But didn't somebody take you in?" asked Dyke indignantly.

"They offered," said Aunt Mathilda, "but we're proud." Then, "We were proud," she amended.

"And the funny thing is," said Wick again, "that we've come to like living in a tent. Like it! Actually! I can't tell what it is, but—"

"It's the rain at night," said Aunt Mathilda, "right by your ear."

"Or the smells first thing in the morning," said Uncle Wick thoughtfully. "*You* know, Dyke, all clean and fresh and—"

"Or the cosiness, maybe," said Aunt Mathilda. "Being all crowded up and cosy."

"No! I know what it is," said Wick with a flash of his old energy. "It's the lack of them *bolts*. That's what it is. Keys, locks, bars, chains, bolts, rattling and clanging and fettering a body in. There's no bolts on a tent, and that's at the heart of the matter. I sleep easy now, without burglars to listen for, and that I've never done before in my whole life."

"We've nothing left to be robbed of, d'ye see," explained Aunt Mathilda.

"I do see, oh, I do," said Dyke. "And a good thing, too. Oh, I'm not saying I'm glad your house burned down," he added hastily, "just that I'm glad it's done some good for you."

"And what will you do now?" asked Hetty, who couldn't help being practical, even at times of the greatest crisis. "Will you build the place up again, Wick, and start over?"

"No!" said Wick, with such decision that the Signposters jumped. "Never!"

"Never!" repeated Aunt Mathilda. "That we *are* sure of."

"I've gone right against candles," said Uncle Wick, and Barley, watching him, thought how strange it was that now he was thinner and his eyes were larger and brighter, he really did look a cut above making candles—the kind of candles he used to go in for, at any rate. "I don't feel as if I shall ever make another."

"Oh come now, Wick," protested Dyke. "A man can't toss away his life's work as if it were no more than a bent farthing!"

"It *is* no more than a bent farthing," said Uncle Wick. "I'm so against candles, that I can hardly bring myself to light one."

Barley remembered that she had once heard Kit use those very words; they reminded her of what she had to say. Before she had time to take in her deep breath and deliver it, all at once, Wick was saying:

"What we thought was that we'd talk it over with the rest of the Family. At Ingle, I mean."

Dyke was staring at Wick in joy and disbelief.

"At Ingle?" he cried at last. "You'll come then, Wick?"

"We'll both come," said Uncle Wick. Then, with a glimpse of his old pomposity, "There's nothing like Family in times of trouble."

"Oh, there isn't, there isn't!" agreed Dyke joyfully, and Hetty, partly because she could see that the hand-wringing and back-slapping was in danger of starting all over again, and partly to hide her own feelings, said:

"Well, then, Matty, now that that's settled, what about setting about some supper? We had a bite ourselves not long back, but I daresay we could all do with another."

Barley watched Aunt Mathilda's face but it showed not a sign of annoyance. A month of tent life had changed her for ever now from a Mathilda into a Matty.

Barley followed them out and helped them make a fire in the brick hearth that Uncle Wick had built with an oven beside it. Aunt Matty was evidently very proud of this, and of her spit, and the tripod for holding her cauldron.

"All made by Wick," she told them. "He's a handy man out of doors."

Her eyes darted past Hetty and Barley to the road beyond, straining in the near darkness.

"Another traveller," she remarked. "Nobody *I* know."

Barley turned, watched the approaching figure for a moment, and then sat down and began to peel potatoes. Then something about the figure, its shape or the way it moved, made her look again, and this time she did not take her eyes away until it was near enough for her to be quite sure. Then she flung her knife to the ground, gathered up her skirts and began to run, stumbling over the heavy earth until she reached him and flung her arms around him, crying, "Kit! Kit! It's you, it's you!"

The scene that followed was impossible to describe. Hetty often tried afterwards but always had to give up.

"It was—it was—" she would begin, "oh, you would never have believed it. You never saw such a sight in your life!"

Everyone began laughing and crying all over again. What Barley remembered most afterwards was the look on Kit's face of delight and pleasure, but a strange look, as if he hadn't expected to be delighted or pleased, and was surprised to find that he was.

When the first storm had died down Barley whispered

to Kit, "What made you come? Have you changed your mind about candles?"

Kit only shook his head, and murmured the one word, "Quill," and Barley was left wondering again at the strangeness of paths crossing and recrossing.

Soon the Wicks and the Signposters were seated round a blazing fire, the stew was simmering and to crown all, the moon was coming up, quite full, perfectly round and satisfied-looking. Dyke looked round the circle with what Barley described as his Family Look—half pride and half purest pleasure.

"This *is* a treat," he said. "What a day this has been."

"Tomorrow'll be a bit flat after, I suppose," said Aunt Matty, who had not lost all her gloom all at once—and nor could she be expected to have done.

"Flat?" said Dyke, his voice rising. "Flat? When we're all off to Ingle? And no more'n a week to the Day? Flat, you say?"

"Well," said Aunt Matty, "now that you put it like that, not flat, exactly. It's just that you can't go expecting good things to happen *all* the time."

"Oh can't you!" cried Dyke recklessly. "*I* do!"

Kit had been quiet for a little while and now he suddenly blurted out, as if it were something he must say at all costs, "I haven't come back to make candles, father. I can't be a candle-maker, I *can't*!"

Uncle Wick looked at him.

"Candle-maker?" he repeated at last, as if the idea had never occurred to him. "Candle-maker? I should think not, indeed."

Kit heard him, but could not believe that he had.

"But, father," he gasped, "you always said—"

Wick put up his hand for silence in one of his old lordly gestures.

"There's been a fire," he said. "You've got me before the fire, and me after. Two entirely opposite Wicks. The things I was used to say and do before the fire, you may forget. Absolutely forget. I'm what you might call a new Wick, and new wicks, to make a proverb, new wicks burn clean!"

# *Chapter Fifteen*

Next morning the Signposters and the Wicks set off on the day-long journey to Ingle. The Wicks had no wagon of their own, so their few belongings were packed into Dyke's, while Kit and Aunt Matty sat up in front with the Signposters, and Uncle Wick himself rode Grayling, his own pony. This surprised everybody, since for many years Wick had refused to visit Pen because he disliked long spells in the saddle. He seemed to like it that day, though. He cantered ahead of them, waving the switch he had cut for himself, and using it to point out things of interest on the road, shouting back to them over his shoulder. They were all things the Signposters had seen twenty times before, but they shouted back to him encouragingly, even after they had become thoroughly tired of it.

It was evening again before they reached Ingle and looked down into the familiar bowl-shaped valley to see Pen's steeple, complete at last, rearing faultlessly into the sky, with the sun's last rays glinting on its brand new weathercock.

"Oh!" cried Hetty, clasping her hands together. "What a beautiful sight! What a downright picture!"

Wick had reined in his horse beside them.

"Did *Pen* do it?" he asked incredulously. "Build that steeple?"

"Of course," replied Hetty. "And steeples isn't easy, either, not like a tower."

"Makes my candles look a bit fiddling," remarked Uncle Wick, sounding wistful.

"*Oh* no it doesn't," said Dyke energetically. "You don't go comparing candles with steeples. If I went comparing my posts with Pen's steeples, I should give up altogether. What's well done is worth doing, post, candle, steeple and all."

He gave Cornish a flick and they began the steep descent into Ingle, the last lap of their long journey. Barley thought that now, more than ever before, it seemed like coming home.

Partly it was because of the way the sunlight flooded the valley in a great golden pool of light. It was all gold and richness, with its round, gleaming haystacks, glittering roofs and quiet fields of gilt-backed sheep. But most of all, it was because through all the long summer months Ingle had come to stand for Family, and soon the Flockshire Smiths would be umbrella'd there together at last.

Kit and Barley jumped down from the wagon near the bottom of the hill and ran forward to find Pen. He was there waiting outside the stone cottage, still wearing his canvas apron because he had been carving the last trumpet-blowing angel above the choir stalls when word had come that the Signposters were approaching.

"Why!" he cried. "Barley, you've brought Kit with you!"

It was a perfect homecoming. Wick got down very stiffly from the weary Grayling, but there was nothing stiff about the way he greeted Pen, or admired the church he had built.

"There's no doubt but what that steeple is a noble bit of building, Pen. Not but what I don't think you fool-hardy, dangling and climbing up there like a jackdaw, aiming to get every bone in your body broke. But it's a fine steeple, and that *can't* be gainsaid."

Then, suddenly, out of the blue, as if the idea had just occurred to him for the first time in his life:

"You could make a candle like a steeple!"

"You could, Wick, you could," agreed Pen.

Wick shook his head as if slightly dazed and afterwards went very quiet and thoughtful.

That night as they all sat round after Pen's turkey supper (chicken seemed a bit grudging for *this* kind of a day, he said) they had a real Family Talk that lasted until midnight. Pen was full of the arrangements for the re-union, and shared them with the Signposters and Wicks—until it came to the matter of the tent.

"The Makers will come the day before," he told them, "and put up the tent in the ten-acre, Dyke, like you said. But oh Dyke, what a tent *that* will be!"

"Tell us about it," begged Barley. "Please, Uncle Pen, describe it to us!"

But Uncle Pen became suddenly mysterious—a thing the Signposters had never known him to be before.

"Oh," he said, "that I couldn't do. Oh no. Oh no."

Nor would he budge, though they tried hard to make him. Barley dreamed all night of tents big as barns and all of scarlet silk, and woke again wondering.

After that, and in the days that followed, there was no time for wondering.

"There's plans to be made," Hetty said, and Pen

*110*

nodded his agreement. They took charge together, while Barley and Dyke scurried round at their bidding, too dazed and excited to do any planning themselves. Dyke in particular often found it necessary to go outside and begin splitting wood for the fire for all he was worth. It was the only way he was able to contain himself, and being a Signposter, contain himself he must.

Pen hung a slate round the neck of one of his stone cocks with a list of all the jobs to be done. Each night he went to it and made a slow satisfying cross by one of the items.

"You wouldn't think there was so much to it!" Dyke would keep saying wonderingly. And "To think it all started as a dream!"

"Dreams need a bit of spadework," Pen told him. "Them that come true do. You've got to help them along."

"I daresay that's true," remarked Wick, who up till now had never had a good word to say either for dreams or those that dreamed them. But the most astounding changes were taking place in him. He was making candles like a madman. Coloured candles, twisted candles, almost impossible candles. He was bent over them night and day and could hardly be persuaded to go to bed.

"Light, light!" he muttered when Aunt Matty begged him to stop. "We must have light!"

"Yes, Wick," she said, "but in the *morning*."

"If you was to make the candles a bit plainer, Wick," suggested Hetty, "you'd get them done a lot quicker. Not but that they twiddles isn't very pretty, but a few plain ones thrown in'd hurry things along a bit."

Uncle Wick lifted his head and glared at her with some of his old spirit.

"You're not saying that a plain candle's the same as a fancy, I hope?" he demanded.

"No, no, of course not, Wick," said poor Hetty. "But the *light's* the same."

"It's nothing of the kind," snapped Uncle Wick, and Barley, for once, was inclined to agree with him.

Kit was actually helping with the candles, rather shame-facedly at first, but with growing enjoyment.

"Not that I'd ever be a candle-maker," he told Barley, "but I should never have guessed there was so much life in a bit of wax."

Even with darkness the work was not done. Pen was carving tiny rockers, one for each family of the Flock-shire Smiths, to take home as mementoes. Dyke was working on a signpost to bear the legend, "To the Flock-shire Smith Reunion". "People might get lost, d'ye see," he had explained apologetically when he first began it. But they knew that he was making the post for a very different reason, and Barley knew that once Michaelmas Day was over it would travel with them in the back of the wagon for the rest of their lives.

Hetty and Pen were the cooks and pored over recipes together, arguing over quantities and choosing cakes. Aunt Matty was to be a cook too, on the day, but not a *choosing* cook. Every now and then Hetty would remember her, and say, "What do you think, Matty?"

Aunt Matty would simply pause for a moment in her weaving (she was making a lot of warm woolly garments for Kit when he went back on the road) and say, "Oh yes, yes, Hetty. Very nice indeed. I'm sure. Quite."

But the thing Barley remembered most afterwards about the days leading up to the reunion, was the ladders. There were ladders everywhere. There were ladders up every haystack, for were there not mattresses to be filled and floors to be strewn? There were ladders to lofts, ladders to gables to hang buntings. There were ladders laced among the apple boughs, of course, because it was the fruit harvest, and the orchards were thronged with eager pickers. Uncle Pen's men were swarming up the longest-legged ladders of all, putting the last touches to his church. Up and down, up and down all day—Barley had never before seen so much busyness or so many ladders. At times when the low sun came slanting from behind the clouds, it even seemed that there were ladders to the sun.

She remembered, too, her own increasing fears as the great day drew nearer. During the long lamplit evenings Dyke would lift his head from his carving and look round at them all, busy at their various tasks. Barley, sometimes catching him thus, grew alarmed. What if he were to become contented, and settle down, now that he had gathered a few of the Family together? Uncle Wick and Aunt Matty had decided to build their new house near Uncle Pen's, and for all she knew Ingle would be half-peopled with the Flockshire Smiths if they decided not to return home after the reunion.

She thought of the fresh nights under the stars and the pear-shaped morning dewdrops on gates and all the weathers and winds of the roads, and shivered at the possibility. "I'm a Signposter," she told herself fiercely, "and so's father. He doesn't *belong* in houses." At times like this she looked round Pen's cosy room with its mats and curtains and leaping fire, and longed for the hard turf, for the cold curtain of the autumn grasses and the lonely, unwavering light of the moon.

She longed, in fact, for Signposting, and conjuring up

*113*

the Flockshire Smiths beneath her private umbrella, she would scowl at them and wish them at the very ends of the earth, from where even Dyke, for all his eagerness, could not summon them.

# Chapter Sixteen

On the eve of the reunion the Signposters did not see the arrival of the Makers, or the tent being put up. Pen had taken them inside his church and was proudly showing them the new eagle lectern and the tapestry screens. Then there was his acorn frieze—"seven hundred and forty-one all told"—and his trumpet-blowing angels with cheeks puffed out as if they were the north wind.

"Now up the steeple," said he, and they all spiralled up the steep stone stairs that grew narrower as they went until at last they stopped, having run out of room altogether.

"You can't get right up the point," said Pen, "naturally."

They crowded around one of the slit windows Pen had built "to let the din of the bells out". Barley, who was the smallest, had her chin on the rough stone of the sill and elbows in a forest all around her, but noticed neither. There was the tent!

It was not scarlet, as she had dreamed, but palest blue, so that you could not miss the embroidery—and that *was* scarlet. The design covered the whole roof of the tent and could only really be seen by looking down on it—the very reason why Pen had brought them up his steeple.

It looked oddly familiar to Barley, who could pick out a shield, a lion, and what looked very like a rocking chair. Underneath were three words that stood out quite clearly but which Barley could not read because they seemed to be in a foreign language.

"Procedere est vivere," she read out.

"Blest if it ain't a coat of arms," said Dyke. "Leastways, it *looks* like a coat of arms."

"It is!" cried Pen, at last able to spill the secret. "A coat of arms for the Flockshire Smiths! D'ye like it? A rocking chair rampant and signpost sinister!"

"A coat of arms!" Hetty went craning forward till she was in danger of falling through the narrow window-slit, for she was very narrow herself. Barley, alarmed, caught hold of Hetty's pinafore strings.

"D'ye like the motto?" Pen went on. " 'Procedere est vivere.' That means—To Go Forward is to Live. Because of the Flockshire Smiths always having been on the move, d'ye see, starting right back with old grandfather Smith. And in particular *you*, Dyke. You never stand still."

"But coats of arms is from the king! You can't go making up coats of arms! Those Makers have gone too far this time, Dyke. It's very pretty, and I don't doubt but what they meant well, but it'll have to come down. Coats of arms is from kings."

Hetty had a very healthy respect for royalty. She had only *heard* about kings, and never actually seen one, so in her deepest heart was not even sure that they were mortal. If she tried to picture Dyke in a crown she never could, and that always seemed to bear out her theory. At any rate, she had a very strong feeling that kings were not to be crossed, and it looked as if the Makers were doing this very thing. She had no time to brood over the matter because Pen was saying with a voice that actually trembled, though it was meant to sound very careless:

"This coat of arms *is* from the king."

No one said anything because the remark was so unexpected and obviously impossible. They just stared dumbly down at the scarlet figured silk and waited for the world to start turning again.

"From the king?" whispered Hetty hoarsely. She did not look honoured. She looked terrified, more than anything.

"His Majesty heard about the reunion, Dyke," said Pen. "He would have come himself, but he broke his legs hunting. He's had a Flock Rocker made into a throne, Dyke. Think of that."

"Just like Grandfather Smith," thought Barley, "when he had *his* accident." She pictured the king restlessly working his gilt Flock Rocker and saw quite clearly that kings were human despite all Hetty's fears.

"I think I'll go down now, Pen," said Wick, "for I think I must sit down. My legs has been taken a little queer."

"Oooh," moaned Aunt Matty, "*my* legs is queer. Let's go down."

They all went down. And still Dyke had not said a word. The Signposters went off by themselves and sat under a hedge to think about it. Hetty was very red and Dyke was very white.

"Well!" said Hetty at last. "A coat of arms. That'll be nice, Dyke."

There was silence.

"Very nice," repeated Hetty. She gave Dyke a nudge.

"Yes," said Dyke.

"We shall be able to have it on the side of the wagon," Hetty went on.

Barley, who so far had not been able to see any real advantages in the honour they had been given, brightened. Now perhaps Hetty would be less particular about fettling the wagon every five minutes. It wouldn't need to be so clean to show everyone they were respectable. People with coats of arms, she supposed, were bound to be more or less respectable, muddy wheels or not.

"Not," went on Hetty, "that we shall go *crowing* about it. Isn't this grass a bit dampish, Dyke? Hadn't we better get up? You know what your bones is like for a bit of damp."

Dyke obediently got up and Hetty flapped the loose wisps of grasses from his breeches with her pinafore.

"You *do* look a bit of a scarecrow, Dyke," she remarked, standing back a little way, hands on hips, surveying him. Luckily at that moment Barley spotted the first wagon rattling into the ten-acre.

"Here they come!" she cried. "Family are coming, father!"

The Signposters craned and stared. They could see the wagon stopping, and then a huddle of figures running towards the pale blue tent. A moment later the first of the Flockshire Smiths were inside it. The reunion had begun.

Dyke threw his Signposter's dignity to the winds. He seized Hetty by the waist and the two of them turned and twirled and stamped in the stubble, staggering between the furrows like lunatics, till Hetty collapsed breathless by the hedge.

"Now look!" she cried. "I shall have to take my boots off. That's what comes of your games, Dyke Signposter."

She untied the laces while Dyke and Barley searched

for sticks. Barley found some, and Dyke came back with a big bunch of berries which he poked behind Hetty's ear. Then all three of them sat scraping the reddish clods from their boots and keeping a sharp eye on the ten-acre as they did so.

"Here's the shepherd and his flock!" cried Hetty. "Lawks! Three wagons! And no wonder."

She stopped suddenly and sniffed.

"Rain!" she said sharply.

Dyke and Barley lifted their heads immediately and scanned the sky. The horizon was a low, purplish blue and the sun came streaming in wide yellow shafts.

"Sun's a bit watery," admitted Dyke grudgingly. "But not *rain*, Hetty."

"*Rain*," she said. She stood up and began to plod off along the hedgerows with her laces still trailing. The others hurried after her. She was never known to be wrong about the weather. All the Signposters could tell a dry spell coming, and scent a thunderstorm, but Hetty could plot a week's weather with a single sniff, or so it seemed to the others.

"Hetty," pleaded Dyke, hurrying after her and tugging at her arm. "Come now, Hetty, not rain. Not *now*."

"Acres of it." Hetty's voice floated back over her shoulder. "Teeming acres."

Barley followed her father and mother, her eyes fixed beyond them on the sky-blue tent. That's *my* dream come true, she thought. An umbrella—or as good as.

# Chapter Seventeen

Nobody slept much that night. Hetty, in predicting rain, had forgotten to mention the wind, and the menfolk, at least, of the Flockshire Smiths had been tugging on ropes and hammering pegs and at times holding the giant tents down to earth with their bare hands. Hetty went out to watch the scene and stood there with her skirts flapping madly and the rain beating on her uncovered head. At last she remarked:

"More rain tomorrow. And if them," nodding her head towards the tents, "takes off, they'll swallow the moon. And they will, I shouldn't wonder."

With this she had gone back inside to grate the nutmeg. She had been disgruntled all evening, and Barley guessed that the reason for this was that her own Family had not yet arrived.

"If he's gone soldiering again," she confided in Barley, "*I'll* give him a battle."

She was beating a bowl of eggs, and they frothed up the sides into a foam that boded ill for Cousin Henry if he had decided to turn absentee again. He still had not arrived by the time Hetty came to bed, and Barley, still lying awake listening to the shouts among the wind and rain, heard her say snappily to Dyke, who had come to fetch the storm lantern:

"You'd best stop up and keep an eye on your Family. Though *some* folk's families stays put, not like other folk's families, that isn't in the same place twice for two weeks put together."

"Now, Hetty," Dyke said soothingly, "he'll be here. He gave his word."

"Word!" she snorted. "More than likely twenty years before there'll be another."

"This reunion's gone amiss." Dyke was glum now. "I didn't bank on wet."

"Wet!" Hetty's voice was brisk again, her own troubles forgotten. "And a good thing too. All the trouble we went to to get them tents. A nice thing if it'd been dry, and no need for them."

With this she pulled together the flaps of the wagon and Barley must have fallen asleep, because when she opened her eyes it was morning. It was only just morning, but already Hetty had dressed and gone out, and there was no sign of Dyke having slept there at all. Remembering that today was the reunion, the day towards which they had been travelling through a whole summer of signposting and dreaming, even as she lay there Barley's heart began to thud. She knelt up and opened the flaps.

The rain was still falling in the grey dawn light, and there was no sign of stir from the quiet acres of the meadow where the two tents still miraculously stood. The wind had dropped. Hastily Barley dressed and with her cloak over her head ran towards Uncle Pen's house, where she guessed the others would be. Pausing by the red and yellow tent, she could hear faint, muffled snores, oddly reassuring in that vast dawn silence.

"They're still here," she exulted, and pictured the

slumbering Flockshire Smiths under the whispering canvas.

Picking her way through the dripping statues in Pen's garden she went into the house and found a state of confusion that was unbelievable. Aunt Matty had burnt two batches of cakes since dawn and was sitting in a Flock Rocker with her pinafore over her head sobbing wildly. Hetty was flying here and there between dangerously balanced trays of cakes and goodies, with the twin red spots on her cheeks that were always signs of danger.

"The lard!" she cried. "Where's the lard?"

"Now keep calm, Hetty, do," said Dyke, himself looking like a scarecrow in his slept-in clothes and muddy boots. "Lard's not the end of the world."

"If there's any here can make pastry without lard, *there's* the bowl," she pointed a dramatic finger, "*there's* the flour, and *there's* the oven!" She looked wildly round her. "Oh, oh, you *can't* make pastry without lard!"

She dropped into a Flock Rocker and up went *her* pinafore over her head. Dyke and Barley stared at each other across the domes of brown sugared buns. Dyke opened his mouth and was about to speak when down came Hetty's apron.

"Where's Pen?" she cried.

"Now, Hetty," said Dyke, "you know as well as I do. He's gone to do an acorn."

"Acorn!" Hetty shrieked. "Acorn! At a time like this!"

"It starts his day off right," said Dyke, and Barley could tell his sympathy was with Pen, out there in the dim quiet of the church peacefully chipping in the day among his own thoughts. She wondered fleetingly whether Uncle Pen would ever be able to *stop* making acorns now that he had got into such a habit of it. She pictured the church in a few years' time, with oak branches twisting up the spire like ivy and acorns spilling out from all the windows, and let out a smothered laugh.

Hetty saw her for the first time. Barley watched her mouth open, and then her eyes travel beyond her to the door and her whole face crumple.

"Cousin Henry!" she cried and burst into tears.

After that, no more pinafores were thrown over heads and the preparations for the party became less frenzied. The Flockshire Smiths left their tents and set off in the rain into Ingle for the Fair. Dyke, Kit and Cousin Henry cleared the sky-blue tent of its mattresses, strewed new straw, and put up trestle tables.

During the afternoon a constant flow of food went out from Pen's kitchen, covered with cloths to protect it from the rain. When at last everything was ready they all went out to survey their handiwork. The trestle tables were arranged from the centre, like the spokes of a wheel, and piled with miniature mountains of food.

"That food'll *never* all get ate!" exclaimed Hetty, delighted by the thought.

They huddled there together in the misty, bluish light of the tent, admiring Wick's candles, Barley's jugs of leaves and berries, Aunt Matty's cut-out doilies. They talked excitedly, but in subdued voices, because of the vastness of the empty tent and the grandeur of the untouched feast.

Whenever Barley thought about the Reunion afterwards, all she could really remember was the *feel* of it. She saw an endless procession of Flockshire Smiths coming into the tent, tired, wet-faced and ordinary, but somehow becoming transformed as they took their places at the long trestles into something that was not ordinary at

all, something that they had never been before, leading
their separate lives in the far reaches of Flockshire. She
could not remember a single word of Dyke's speech,
either. He had stood on a box in the centre by the tent
pole, and she remembered only the spoking rows of
listening Smiths with their eager, upturned faces, and
they always blurred into the same pale wheel about

her, and she supposed that this, at last, was Family Feeling.

Hetty, who had a much smaller Family to give her attention to, was the one who could be relied on to remember the details.

"Pen's quince candies went first," she would say musingly, "which I would never have reckoned on. And who would've thought those apple rings would've got ate so fast? You'd have thought they'd never *seen* an apple. But your speech was a treat, Dyke. You could tell that, the way they banged their plates on the table at the end. Not but what it isn't bad *manners* banging plates on tables," she added. "I was brought up to stamp feet, not bang plates."

"Stamping feet on straw don't do very much, Hetty," Dyke would point out mildly, and Hetty would usually concede the point, adding, "I *like* a bit of noise at a feast, anyhow."

Once the trestles had been cleared away and the fiddlers struck up, there was plenty of noise that night. But again, strangely enough, Barley's main memories were of the silences, in which you could hear, above the spluttering of candles, shuffling of straw and munching of jaws, the rain pattering on the darkening roof of the tent, drawing the Flockshire Smiths the closer under the umbrella of Barley's own dream.

When at last it was all over, and the Signposters went out from the warm, steamy tent into the fresh night air, the rain, miraculously, had stopped, and the moon was out.

They wandered home, dazed, across the wet meadow, in the greenish silver light. Then all at once Dyke stopped. For a long while none of them spoke.

"Aaaah!" Dyke drew in a deep breath of the chill night air. "Aaaaaaah!" again.

"I know," agreed Hetty, following suit.

They stood, the three of them, contentedly breathing in and feeling part of the night, as near to it as a stoat or badger, for they had known it as well and twice as long.

In the growing silence Barley was curiously aware that

the tide of the year had turned, that they had at last gone over the brow of the hill. There would be a brief pause, and then the old rhythm of Signposting would begin again, the familiar pattern of roads and winds and weathers that would lead them again towards the winter, and full circle.

Dyke, clearing his throat, voiced her own thoughts.

"Well, then, Hetty and Barley," he said. "That rounded off the season nicely."

"It did," agreed Hetty. "And Dyke, we've stood here long enough. We shall all end up with damp in our bones."

And they padded silently home past the sleeping Flock-shire Smiths under the moonlit umbrella, keeping close to the hedge as a weasel does, or a fox.

# Epilogue

After the Family Reunion the Signposters took the road again without the least change in their lives except that now their wagon bore the crest of the Flockshire Smiths, emblazoned on the sides by the Lamfrey Makers. The Makers themselves thereafter marked all their work with the crest, so if you have any very old ginger-spotted pottery cats or out-of-the-way paper weights, I should turn them upside down and have a closer look.

As for Uncle Wick, he stayed a candle-maker, of course. He had to, because as Dyke pointed out, a man can't throw away his life's work because of a fire. All his candles burned away long ago, but it is a pity you could not have seen them. He stayed in Ingle and made candles like steeples, candles curled and coloured and never two the same. Kit went to London and became a famous actor, and Pen built three more churches—if you visit Ingle you can see them still.

But the Family Reunion did a strange thing. It stirred up the wanderlust in the Flockshire Smiths. It was as if once they had started travelling again they could not stop. Soon they were peopling the length and breadth of England—impossible to visit on pacings and not what poor Dyke had intended at all.

There is no wonder, then, that nowadays the telephone directories are so full of Smiths. If *your* name is Smith, and you find it difficult to stay put in one place for very long, it might be worth your while to pay a visit to Somerset House and look up your family tree. You might find that you are entitled to head your notepaper with a rocking chair rampant and signpost sinister. Not to mention the Latin motto, "Procedere est vivere," which has the virtue, as Dyke often used to say, of being perfectly true.